Cristina & T. J.

I wish you best in life.

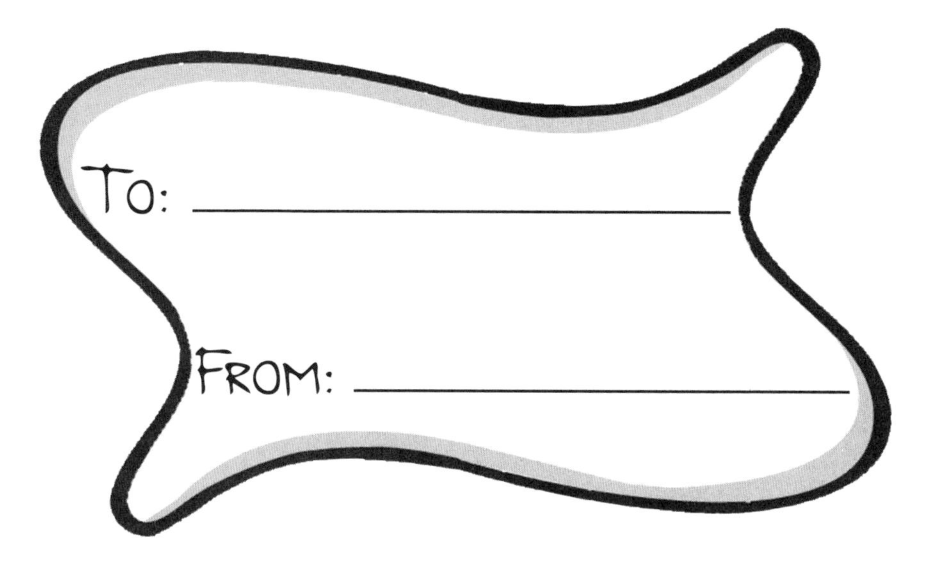
To: ______________________
From: ______________________

I Wanna Be...

John Jacobs
with Daniel Jacobs

Cameo Publications, LLC

06 07 08 09 10 HH 5 4 3 2 1
First Edition
Printed in the United States of America
ISBN 10: 0-9774659-6-9
ISBN 13: 978-0-9774659-6-5
BISAC - JUV039140
Library of Congress Control Number: 2006925376
$9.99 U.S. Funds

A portion of the proceeds from the sale of this book go to the Sandy Stockings Foundation to help people fulfill their dreams. For more information please go to: ***www.sandystockings.com***

Cover & Interior Design by Amanda Finney, Cameo Publications, LLC.

Distributed through the services of Cameo Publications.

Dedication

This book is dedicated to you, dear reader, and to all of the Sandys and Ashers in the world – those who know deep down inside themselves that they are not dumb or ugly just because they are what people call "different." You don't have to be what society calls brilliant, popular, rich or good-looking to be perfect. Your creativity, inner intelligence, and spirit are what make you who you are and what make you perfect.

If you feel like it's just too much sometimes, you're not alone. But you can't retreat inside yourself, or you'll never reach your full potential. If you feel stuck in a "wannabe" state of mind, thinking that you just don't deserve what you truly desire or don't have what it takes to be what you most want to be, that's about to change!

I sincerely believe every child or young adult has all the ability to learn and achieve everything they've dreamed of. So, dear reader, if you haven't heard it lately – or ever – *we are proud of you! You are beautiful and smart.* Now *be proud of* yourself! *And get ready to become that which you truly are!*

May your journey with Sandy in this first book of her Saga be a *great* one. Remember to Become, Be Near, and Be Ready to be what *you* wanna be!

Sincerely,

John Jacobs

I Wanna Be...

Dance as though no one is watching you,
Love as though you have never been hurt before,
Sing as though no one can hear you,
Live as though Heaven is on Earth.

~ Souza

"The road to success is not straight. There is a curve called Failure, a loop called Confusion, speed bumps called Friends, red lights called Enemies, caution lights called Family. You will have flats called Jobs. But, if you have a spare called Determination, an engine called Perseverance, you will make it to a place called Success."

~ Author Unknown

Chapter One

Certain things in certain houses never see the light. Secrets, sad memories, and sometimes a whole person manage to weave in and around conversations, never destined to be brought up. These certain things in these certain houses can go years without ever seeing light.

Sandy lived in one of these certain houses, and Sandy's father happened to be one of these certain things. She didn't really know what had happened; she just knew that he was dead. Her mother never talked about it, and the few times Sandy mentioned anything about him, her mother would turn, walk up the stairs, and crawl into bed. Whether or not she was actually sleeping never crossed Sandy's mind.

Most people who knew Sandy's mother, Mrs. Stockings, described her as an "artist," a "very passionate person," or simply "an actress." When they'd call her these things, it wasn't said respectfully, but usually with a superior wink or an exaggerated tone of voice, as if they were making fun of her a little bit. People seemed to think they could sum up who she was, explain Mrs. Stockings' whole story, with those terms.

From an early age, Sandy knew that her mother was different from other mothers. She'd once asked a neighbor, Mrs. Debrah, if all grown ups slept as much as her mother did.

Mrs. Debrah responded nervously, "Your mother, dear, is… well, a *very passionate person*… she's, she's an *artist*… you see, sweetie… your mother is an *actress*."

Sandy noted that, though she had heard all of the terms before, and with the same pronunciation, Mrs. Debrah was the only person to ever use all three in one explanation. Mrs. Debrah didn't help Sandy to understand, but she did make her feel better—like her mother was special somehow.

She could remember when her mom wasn't tired all the time. Once, she'd cook big meals and would laugh at Sandy's jokes and Sandy's father's stories about his day. After dinner, the three of them would make up little plays and act them out, making capes from bed sheets and turbans from towels. When she was very little, Sandy might sit in the bathtub for two hours, talking with her mom or dad about her dreams, asking questions, and listening to their advice and plans for the future. All that seemed like it happened a million years ago now.

Her mother moved slowly out of the kitchen, sipping a reheated cup of coffee. She was still wearing her pink bathrobe, and through the door, Sandy saw boxes full of her mother's memories lying around the living room, a sign that Mrs. Stockings had had a bad day.

Sandy microwaved a hot dog and brought it into the living room, clearing a place on the couch next to her mother. As

Chapter One

Mrs. Stockings listlessly flipped the pages of a yearbook, Sandy looked at her mother with her studying eyes. She pictured her mother as she used to look on a Saturday night, with a little make-up on, when she was going out for a special night with Sandy's dad. She used to smell like perfumed powder, and she'd dot Sandy's nose with her puff to make her giggle. She was so beautiful, with her sparkly earrings and perfect smile. She'd look over her shoulder as they left the house and whisper to Sandy, standing with the sitter, "I love you. Be a good girl."

Mrs. Stockings knew her daughter was remembering better times, and it broke her heart to see such disappointment. She tried to smile at Sandy, but she couldn't hold onto it, so instead she looked away, stood up from the couch, and ascended the stairs to her room. "I'm going to sleep," she called down. "Don't stay up too late."

Sandy sat alone, looking around the living room at the boxes her mother had unearthed from their various hiding spots. The biggest box was full of memorabilia from her acting career. Friends and old flames filled five smaller boxes. But the metal lock box was Sandy's favorite. This box was full of all her mother's embarrassing secrets from middle school to high school.

The boxes were full of old pictures, letters, or wrinkled playbills advertising the various roles of the once-famous Estelle Stockings. Since her father died four years before, Sandy had seen whole weeks go by when her mother did nothing but sleep and remember, like she was stuck. This happened slowly at first. For a couple of years after Sandy's father's death, Mrs. Stockings still held a job, but then she gradually stopped shopping for groceries or for clothes for Sandy, and she never cleaned the house.

"I'm just too tired," she'd say in her sad, raspy voice, about practically everything, and Sandy had learned pretty quickly to fend for herself with a little help from Mrs. Debrah. Nobody else really came around anymore, either, including the kids in the neighborhood she used to play with. It was just Sandy and her mom now. Every month, a life insurance payment kept the bills paid, and one of Sandy's chores became riding her bike to the grocery whenever all the food ran out.

It was weird that her mother had left the memory boxes sitting out. Usually, when she had spent the day remembering, Sandy wasn't even allowed into the house until all of the boxes were tucked safely away into their hiding places. But Sandy knew where to look—she'd been through all of the boxes five or six times. She had read every journal cover to cover until she knew the stories behind all the photos, the situations discussed in every letter, and her mother's rating of every performance of her stage career. If the facts behind certain photographs weren't in the journals or the letters, Sandy made up stories for her mother to take part in. After a while, these became just as real to her as the rest.

The first few times, Sandy looked through her mother's memories to try to understand what had happened to her father. She knew there had been some kind of accident, but as soon as her mother got the phone call, Sandy had been shipped to an aunt's house for a couple of weeks, didn't go to the funeral, and couldn't remember much even of what she'd overheard since then. It was a big blank spot, and the person who could paint the picture would never, ever do it.

Chapter One

She'd found no answers in her mother's boxes, no pictures of her father, no love letters or ticket stubs, or evidence of any kind that he'd ever existed, except in her own memories. All proof of her father's part in their lives seemed to be wrapped solely within Sandy now. One day, she'd just decided to start over again, focusing all of her attention on the one parent she still had, though many days, she felt like an orphan.

Still, plenty of times when she was falling asleep, she'd remember her father sitting by her bed reading to her before she fell asleep. He'd given her a little stuffed bee one time, and he'd fly it in slow circles over her head, pretending the bee was telling her a story. The movements and the sound of his deep voice always hypnotized her, and she couldn't help but nod off, no matter how hard she tried to stay awake.

One summer day, she took the bee with her to a patch of woods near her house where she would "fly free," as her father used to call it, and accidentally left the bee behind. She went back the next day, but the toy was nowhere to be found. She'd give anything to have it back now, she thought.

Sometimes, when she was day-dreaming in school, which is how she spent almost all of her time there, if she'd concentrate extra-hard, she could hear her father's voice, or even feel his hand on her shoulder. On weekends and after school, she used to get far away from everyone and everything, going back to the special place where she used to "fly free." She'd sit on a log talking to him. But now it seemed like so much time had passed that she couldn't remember his face or voice very well, and she hardly even believed he was listening anymore. Sometimes she'd still make the effort, but she just felt...empty.

I Wanna Be...

As Sandy got down on her knees to shop through the various boxes, something new caught her eye. A velvet bag lay open under the coffee table. Sandy crawled over and moved her hand along the outside of the bag. She felt strange finding something new that could, in fact, be something very old. She took her time, approaching cautiously, like a visitor hesitates to pet an unfamiliar dog.

As she reached inside the bag, she felt several framed pictures and a single photo without a frame. She pulled the photo out, hands trembling a little, and turned it over and to see the eyes of a man whose face had for years now lived only in her dreams.

Flipping the portrait over, she stared at the smudged name on the back for a long time: John Robert Stockings. She said the name over and over in her head, then turned the picture over again. Though it was black and white, she could see how much darker her father's hair was than her own or her mother's.

Sandy felt dizzy, as the familiar ball of fire began to grow in her stomach. She had to think about breathing in, breathing out. Her chest felt painfully tight, as though something was trying to explode out of it. She concentrated on steadying her hands, and placed the picture face up on the ground beside her.

Slipping her hand inside the bag again, she grasped a thick object, solid but soft, with a smooth surface. Just as she started to pull it from the bag, she heard her mother's door open upstairs.

She jerked her hand out of the bag, saw that it was clutching some kind of book, and managed to stuff the book under a couch cushion behind her before her mother had reached the stairs. Shoving the picture back into the bag, she tried to rearrange the bag as it was before she found it.

Mrs. Stockings walked into the room, looking more rumpled than usual and a little startled, as though she'd suddenly woken up and wasn't quite sure where she was.

"Have you been rummaging around in my things, Sandy?" Mrs. Stockings asked in a low voice, rubbing her eyes.

"No, ma'am," Sandy said.

"It's all right to tell me the truth, Sandy. Have you been rummaging through your mother's boxes?" Her careful phrasing had a stern undertone.

"I was just about to, but you came down before I really got started," Sandy said with a slightly guilty laugh she hoped her mother would believe.

"I don't know why I bother hiding any of it," Mrs. Stockings muttered. "It's only about me..." But she stopped just as she spotted the bag under the table. Sandy saw her, and acted as though she hadn't noticed it. Mrs. Stockings gave Sandy a hard look, and continued, "Tell me, dear, would you rather look through the boxes more or the bag?"

Sandy smiled. Her mother's trick was clever, and had she not already seen the photo, she would definitely have said the bag. "Huh? What bags? All I've seen here are boxes," Sandy answered innocently.

Mrs. Stockings smiled so honestly that Sandy felt a bit of shame for lying, but she knew that if she didn't, her mother would have checked the bag thoroughly. This bought her at least a day with her stolen treasure.

While Sandy thought these things over, her mother seemed

to be doing some plotting of her own. Out of nowhere, Mrs. Stockings said brightly, "Would you mind taking the trash out to the street?"

Aghast, Sandy asked, "All of it?"

"Well…sure…yes, as much as you can," Mrs. Stockings answered, looking anxiously from the coffee table to Sandy.

"That could take a whole *day*, Mother!" Sandy shrieked. Neither of them had taken the garbage to the street in months. Sandy hadn't even bought any more trash bags to replace the ones that ran out in the middle of the summer. Food and other trash was either still decaying on plates in the kitchen or thrown haphazardly into the backyard on top of the mountain of black plastic trash boulders. Even if Sandy could manage to move all of the trash bags from the backyard to the street, no truck would come by to haul it off. Because they hadn't put out any trash for pick up in so long, their house had been taken off the garbage truck's route.

"All right," Mrs. Stockings sighed. "If you're sure you can't tackle the garbage, then at least leave your poor mother alone here for five brief minutes. Go play or something, and then you can come back, and we'll pick our way through some of these memories together. Is that fair?"

Sandy nodded and walked around the couch, passing by her mother who was still watching the coffee table, as if it might come alive and jump out of the nearest window. Sandy moved out the kitchen door toward her favorite sitting steps, but stopped to look back and see her mother kick the bag underneath the couch. Sandy was relieved to see that her mother evidently didn't notice the difference in its weight.

Chapter One

Staring out at the dusk, Sandy thought about the picture of her father and wondered what might be in the book she had found that was so important to her mother that she didn't want Sandy to see it.

A few minutes later, her mother called her in and Sandy sat down on the couch cushion, impatiently longing for what lay beneath her. Her mother, meanwhile, pulled out pictures and letters, digging through her past with mounting excitement and a little of her old animation.

Both of them began to see, though in very different ways, that sometimes certain things in certain houses are destined for the light.

Chapter Two

The poster had too much glitter on it, enough gold dust to fill three lockers. Glitter was glued to glitter. It came off in clumps when students passed by, making the eighth grade hall a mess. The paper was a hideous purple and looked as though it might collapse under the weight of all the glue and sparkle. A dry erase marker had been used to draw thick black lines around the letters. The sign read:

THE DRAMA CLUB
PRESENTS TRYOUTS FOR
THE SPRING PLAY
OCTOBER 14

I Wanna Be...

Sandy stood straight in front of the sign, her nose just inches away from the wall, reading the words over and over again. She didn't need glasses – she had perfect vision –but she couldn't bring herself to walk away. For some reason, she felt as if something had drawn her to this very spot. Why else would a sixth grader as small as Sandy be standing in the eighth graders' hall by herself? She had left class claiming she needed a drink of water, but in reality she was looking for a way to be alone in the hall.

She liked to be alone, most of the time. It felt more natural to her than being in a crowd of people. She'd never been exactly the most popular kid in class, but she used to have some kids to hang around with when she wanted to. But since her dad died, they had all fallen away, like losing a father might be contagious, and some of them had turned on her, trying to bully her before she bullied them.

Though she'd made it to middle school, she had the worst grades in her class and had supposedly caused more trouble than "ten troubled teens," in the words of her elementary school principal, Mr. Hutchins. But the middle school world was completely different from the relative safety of elementary school. Sandy felt as if she were being dragged into the real world.

The year before, fifth grade, had felt pretty good. For the first time in her school career, she had only felt lonely, which was much better than feeling lonely and scared. In fifth grade, no one got to lord their superiority over her. She had been at the top of the food chain, at least in terms of seniority, in elementary school, but now she was thrown right back down with the other bottom feeders of middle school.

Chapter Two

The worst part about being a sixth grader was that everybody seemed to hate sixth graders. The teachers said that they got more and more disrespectful every year. The seventh graders used them as scapegoats for everything bad that happened: soggy meat in the cafeteria, no soda in the machine, Monday's, etc. All the fault of the sixth graders. And the eighth graders treated them as they remembered being treated when *they* were in the sixth grade, which wasn't very good.

Even worse, while it was true that nobody liked the sixth graders, it was also true that nobody hated the sixth graders more than the sixth graders themselves. The bullying was constant, as everyone looked for a weaker kid to put down so they'd maybe feel better about themselves. It seemed like everyone needed a "loser" to exclude, a "dork" to make fun of, and sometimes, someone to shove, just so they could feel superior for a little while

Sandy wanted to be an actress when she grew up, and despite the fact that she wanted more than anything to be in the spring play, she knew that it was social suicide to have anything to do with the Drama Club. She had enough trouble fitting in to add "Drama Geek" to the long list of stuff everyone made fun of her for. She was short for her age, barely coming up to the light switch on the wall, and skinny. She had long red hair that tangled into knots every morning, no matter how many times she brushed it before going to bed. And her face was fully freckled, which meant old people called her "cute," but her many tormentors called her "Freckle Butt," "Spotty," or just plain "Ugly."

None of Sandy's clothes matched, and she couldn't remember the last time she'd gotten something new. Everything she wore was a hand-me-down from her neighbor, Mrs. Debrah, who had eight boys. Sandy always had to wear their old blue jeans or overalls. She didn't own a single dress that fit anymore.

This particular Monday, Sandy was wearing her favorite pair of Erik's overalls (he was the fourth son), Phil's red flannel shirt (he was the second son), and Tom's very first pair of brown leather cowboy boots; they used to have spinning spurs on the heel, but she'd had to take the spurs off the first day of middle school. A hall monitor heard her boots jangling and thought Sandy might use the spurs as a weapon. Sandy sighed, thinking about what had once been the coolest part of her costume.

Just as she was about to return to class, the bell rang. She'd stayed too long daydreaming–something she was often guilty of–about the play. The rumble that followed sounded as though someone had awakened a village of giants. The floor shook under the weight of a hundred anxious eighth graders pouring out of their classes and down the halls toward Sandy. She froze in the spot where she was standing as the giants moved all around her, some of them nice enough to alter their paths, but most of them not noticing and bumping into her.

The star basketball player stepped on her left boot, just as one of the class clowns hit her in the back of the head with his book bag as he walked by. She already felt short among the other sixth graders, but this was different. Now it seemed like she didn't even exist, and she had mixed feelings about that. Because people seemed to ignore her, usually, she was used to feeling invisible; being noticed actually bothered her more.

But then she heard the thunderous stomping of a certain pair of cold, rubber work boots clomping each individual tile

Chapter Two

and coming to a stop right behind her. She knew that clomping all too well.

"Well, well, well. Look who's here in our hall: Teeny-Weeny-Wittle-San-Dee Sock-Stinks!"

"Hello, Clyde," Sandy said through clenched teeth, without even turning around. Clyde was Mrs. Debrah's youngest son, but he was almost twice as tall as Sandy and the strongest boy in his class. He was also Sandy's sworn enemy.

"Whad-a-ya say, Sock-Stinks? What're you doin' in *my* hall?" Clyde said loudly enough for people to take notice. Clyde never did anything without getting others to notice. He didn't like Sandy, and he hated giving her his old clothes. Not that she liked getting them; his hand-me-downs were all black and smelled like bologna.

Clyde's whole life centered around two things: football and fighting. Fighting actually had a lot to do with why he loved football so much. It was the only sport he was good at where hurting people was acceptable.

Students started gathering around, and Clyde's confidence grew. He knew that Sandy never backed down from a fight, and she had that short temper peculiar to many small individuals and redheads. As much as he didn't like Sandy, he did like knowing he could always count on her for a fight.

"It's *Stockings*, Clyde, Sandy *Stockings*," she said, still glaring at the poster on the wall.

"What's this you're looking at, Sock-Stinks? Did you think it was an ad for some more free clothes? Or are you thinkin' bout bein' in the Spring Play?" Clyde snickered. "That'd be just about perfect for you, wouldn't it? Wasn't your crazy Mama an actress?

I mean, ya know, before she went nuts?" Clyde's voice rose a little as he struggled to contain his big, ugly hyena laugh..

Sandy noticed that everyone had stopped what they were doing to look at her. She could feel the blood rushing into her cheeks, and her hands balling up into fists. She knew she had to do something, but she didn't want to get into any trouble the second week of school. But before fully thinking this last point out, Sandy whirled around and punched Clyde as hard as she could in the stomach. She was so fast that nobody had a chance to jump, especially not Clyde, who was forced to take a step back from the blow.

Sandy walked a step forward, and pointed a long, threatening finger up to his face. Clyde regained his composure, but taking the hit had hurt his pride, so he hesitated.

"Listen to me, Clyde Deb-Rah! You shut up about my mother! You have no right to talk about her like that! The only reason you make fun of *my* last name is 'cause *yours* is Debrah, and everyone knows that Debrah's a girl's name, you big stupid *sissy*!" Sandy took a deep breath, as more people circled in to see what was going on.

Clyde noticed the growing audience, and brought his fists into the air, ready to pounce on Sandy.

But she kept right on yelling at him. "And if you want your gross old clothes back, you're gonna have to fish 'em out of the river, 'cause that's where I pitched 'em the second you gave 'em to me, crying to your mama like the little girl you are." Sandy paused, her face still rigid with anger.

Clyde dropped his hands to his side and gave a clever smile, which seemed to pass from one spectator to the next like an electrical current.

Sandy could tell she was losing favor with the crowd and needed to think of something quickly. "And no, I'm not gonna be in the stupid Spring Play, 'cause everybody knows that the Drama Club is just a bunch of geeks who don't have any friends and can't even act. So if you have to know everything, Clyde Deb-Rah, I was just looking at the poster because it is so disgusting that it reminded me of your face!"

Sandy's heart was pounding, and she could feel the hot blood in her cheeks. She hadn't noticed the uncanny silence that had overtaken the crowd of spectators. The smiles of the crowd had clamped into the lip-biting of barely suppressed laughter. Everyone seemed to be looking behind Sandy, just over her shoulder.

Then she heard the noise that sent her pounding heart careening down to her stomach: "Huh-hem."

The pointed clearing of a throat had to belong to the one person on the face of the Earth Sandy didn't want to see. She tried for a second to disappear, but knew she had to turn around and face her math teacher, Ms. Carla Bridgewater.

Though she was still a young woman, Ms. Bridgewater wore thick oval glasses, long wool business suits, and black hair pulled tightly into a bun. "I'm very sorry, Ms. Stockings, that you find my poster so… what was it? 'Disgusting'?" she said in her deadpan voice.

Sandy couldn't believe what was happening. Out of all the people who could have walked by right then, it had to be Ms. Bridgewater! Not only was she the strictest teacher in the sixth-grade, but she was also the head of the whole drama department—including the high school's!

"I... I... I didn't mean anything by it, Ms. Bridgewater," Sandy said quietly.

"I'm sure you didn't," Ms. Bridgewater said, but Sandy didn't think she looked like she was very sure. "Still, that's not important right now, is it? Mr. De-Bray, what is going on here?"

Sandy had noticed since the first week of middle school that for some reason Clyde was Ms. Bridgewater's favorite student, even though he wouldn't be caught dead in a play. And whenever she said his last name, she always split it up into two parts and added an accent to the end to make it sound French and sophisticated.

Clyde was attempting to hide his satisfaction at the events that had suddenly turned in his favor. "I was just asking lil' Sandy here if she thought she'd be interested in trying out for our school play. I knew I was going to, and I thought I could help encourage some of my fellow students to do the same. I don't know what got into my lil' neighbor here, but she just started yellin' and punched me in the gut." Clyde couldn't say the word "lil'" without patting Sandy on the head.

Sandy looked up at Ms. Bridgewater, hoping she wouldn't buy Clyde's story. She was horrified to see that the teacher not only seemed to be buying it, but also seemed downright overjoyed that Clyde was going to try out for her play.

Ms. Bridgewater loomed over Sandy, shaking her head wearily. "Very well, Mr. De-Bray. I should have known who started this kind of trouble. On a lighter note, however, it will be a *pleasure* seeing you on the stage this October." Ms. Bridgewater beamed at Clyde with such maternal satisfaction that Sandy thought Clyde's own mother would have been put to shame.

Clyde was quick to respond. "That's the thing, though, ya see, I realized after I told lil' Sandy about the play, that I'm not gonna be able to try out this year, 'cause I made the Varsity football team, and their season starts next month, so I'd have to miss the performance."

Clyde's disappointed pout didn't fool any of his fellow eighth graders, but Ms. Bridgewater seemed convinced, though she didn't like hearing it. She often said that too many great actors were lost to athletics, and for some reason she scowled down at Sandy as though Sandy were to blame for Clyde's preference for pummeling over performing. "I'm very sorry that Ms. Stockings resorted to violence against you, Mr. De-Bray," she said. "Perhaps she'll learn her lesson when she and I are forced to spend the entire afternoon together in detention."

Clyde smiled triumphantly at Sandy, and ruffled her hair again as he said, "Oh, please, Ms. Bridgewater, don't blame lil' Sandy here on my account. I'd hate to think that I was the one that got her into trouble. I was just trying to help her because she's dis-ad-VAN-taged," he added softly and meaningfully, as if he were a counselor, or Ms. Bridgewater's concerned peer. Sandy just stood there, but she wanted to hit him over and over and over again.

"How thoughtful of you, Clyde, but I'm afraid Ms. Stockings is going to have to learn that she can't go flying off the handle whenever she feels like it," Ms. Bridgewater said calmly. Then, turning to Sandy, she cleared her throat again, sharpened her eyes, and muttered, "I'll see you in my office at three o'clock this afternoon."

Ms. Bridgewater turned and walked away, her heels clicking down the tile hall. The eighth graders dispersed at the sound of the next bell, all of them talking loudly about the weird unknown sixth grader who'd been wandering around their hall. Sandy stayed behind, trying not to hear the giggling giants as they passed her.

When the second bell rang, she found herself completely alone. She turned around and stared one last time at the purple poster, noticing that the top was beginning to creep forward. The right corner came completely off the wall and began to sag, gradually pulling the left corner loose, too. Sandy felt no impulse to do anything, but merely watched the sign fall to the ground and explode into a cloud of gold dust that covered the legs of her overalls. Sandy looked down at her pants, and said, "That poster *did* have too much glitter on it."

Chapter Three

When she opened the door to Ms. Bridgewater's office at 3:00, Sandy smelled a combination of dusty clothes, wet newspaper, and stale coffee, with a little fresh paint and cat litter thrown in.

Ms. Bridgewater called it an office, but the room contained no desk, carpet, chairs, or window. Solid metal filing cabinets, loose papers, and water-stained scripts filled the room, and costumes hung everywhere. Victorian dresses and stiff men's suits lined the right coat rack, while colorful islander clothes were draped over the higher water pipes. Blazers and tuxedo jackets hung from the air conditioner duct, and fuzzy ape costumes were balled up on a shelf. Pirate hats bedecked with the skull and crossbones sat next to toy pistols. Dozens of swords, some broken and some stained, slumped in a box filled with plastic plates made to look like fine china.

Sandy stood transfixed, taking in the scene with such pleasure that she forgot why she was there. She remembered the little shows she would put on with her mom and dad and thought how much more fun it would be to use these cool things to tell a story than the bath towels and broomsticks they had used. Still, they had fun…

She was startled to hear the door open behind her, and turned quickly, feeling guilty about relaxing and imagining for a minute, to see Ms. Bridgewater in the doorframe. Neither of them said anything.

At last, feeling incredibly awkward, Sandy said, "I was just looking at all this great stuff you have."

"Well, don't get too comfortable in here, Ms. Stockings. You're here because you've gotten yourself into some more trouble," Ms. Bridgewater said, moving closer to Sandy. "Your reputation preceded you. I had quite a long talk with your former principal, Mr. Hutchins. He lets us know the names of problem children we need to keep an eye on, and now here we are. I've been watching you closely, and I find you to be remarkably like your mother—too much so, perhaps." Ms. Bridgewater stared at Sandy with unwavering eyes.

Sandy had shuddered at the way her teacher pronounced her name, with contempt, but when Ms. Bridgewater brought her mother up, she felt the same furious energy inside her as when Clyde had made fun of her "crazy mama."

"What do you know about my mother?" Sandy asked with as much threat in her voice as she could manage with an adult.

"I have known your mother for many years," Ms. Bridgewater replied, clearly not sensing any danger from Sandy. "We were in the same theatre workshops a long time ago. She was always very pretty. And your father, of course, very handsome."

Chapter Three

She stopped and smiled strangely.

Sandy went pale, and felt as though she were going to be sick. "You knew him, too? My father?"

"Everyone thought so highly of him," Ms. Bridgewater went on. "We were all quite jealous of Estelle, when he finally married her." She smiled slightly, but with a faraway look in her eye. "Although maybe we should be thankful—such a pity what happened. To die so young. I cannot even begin to imagine."

Sandy was now breathing very heavily. She knew people wanted to see weakness at times, and she didn't want to give Ms. Bridgewater anything she might be looking for. It wasn't like she could sock her teacher in the stomach, but she wanted to do something to not feel as bad as she did all of a sudden. She mustered up all of her courage to casually continue their conversation, trying to shift it to some other–any other–subject.

"I'd like to be an actress. I've always dreamed about coming in here," she blurted before thinking. As soon as the words were out of her mouth, she blushed. I really am an idiot, she thought.

"No doubt you did this dreaming in my class," Ms. Bridgewater said with raised eyebrows. "But I'm afraid theatre has a requirement, which you seem to lack, and that is self-discipline. I've just graded your first quiz, Ms. Stockings, and I must say your performance was not inspiring."

Ms. Bridgewater moved over to a box of dresses covered in lint. She picked up one of the dirtier dresses and lightly brushed it with the palm of her hand, then turned to look at Sandy. "I need this room cleaned and organized. Figure out how things are categorized in here and clean it up. Understood? That will be your only task for today."

Sandy didn't say anything, but merely looked around the cluttered room. What had just appeared magical to her moments ago now seemed much darker and overwhelming. This was as bad as having to haul the garbage bags from the backyard. "It would take all week to get a dump like this organized," she whined.

"It certainly might, Ms. Stockings," Ms. Bridgewater said sharply.

Sandy looked up quickly, not realizing she had been thinking out loud, a dilemma she often found herself in, now that she spent so much time alone.

"And if that is the case," Ms. Bridgewater continued, "you will return every day after school until the task *is* accomplished. You will find the cleaning supplies in the closet by the girl's bathroom. The school is locked at precisely five o'clock each day. I'll be down the hall in my classroom if you have any questions." And then she left the room, closing the door behind her.

Sandy watched the door for a very long time, half expecting it to open back up to reveal Ms. Bridgewater's scornful look. For a minute, she wondered why Mrs. Bridgewater seemed to hate her so much, and then she started thinking about all the teachers she had gone through. The only thing they seemed to have in common was that she had never learned anything from any of them.

Staring at the door, she thought about better times, before she had to go to school, when she had still had her family. She thought about her mother who had taught Sandy the alphabet and how to read using the various plays she had been in. She remembered her father giving her money and teaching her how to count. Everything that she had ever learned was in her head before she stepped into her first classroom. And since then, it seemed like all school had done was make her feel stupid and even smaller than she was, small *inside*. A feeling in the pit of her stomach grew upward until her chest hurt.

She focused on the door in front of her, and tried to lose herself inside her mind. Sandy had the ability to "zone out" as her mother said, "daydream" as her teachers said, or "go into a coma" as her classmates said. Whatever happened to her, it could last a few minutes or a few hours. She became the very definition of "lost in thought."

Staring off into the distance for as long as she felt like, she needed nothing to entertain her. She knew exactly what was in her mind, and yet, at the same time, she had no idea. If someone asked her if she was thinking, she would answer "yes." But if they asked her what she was thinking *about*, she never knew a good answer, so she'd respond, "Nothing." She found herself zoning out in all of her classes. The progress of a ladybug walking across the room on the floor captivated more of her attention than the most eloquently delivered school lesson. Not that there were many of those. Sandy hated school, or at least she really, really didn't like it. School was boring, and she never learned anything.

By the time she'd gotten to the fifth grade, most of Sandy's teachers didn't even bother trying anymore. She was known as "a problem child," and they were glad to be rid of her at the end of each year. For the most part, her teachers always let her get away with the stupid things she did, as if everyone just expected trouble from her, so her punishments didn't come along with lectures about "disappointment" or "wasted potential." She knew she wasn't letting anybody down by throwing a rock at the boy that called her "Sand-pee." And no one was shocked when she failed another quiz, or didn't do her homework. She was considered the "dumb one" in her grade, and everyone accepted it—including Sandy.

Every year, her teachers expressed the same concerns at parent-teacher conferences. Sandy started looking at the meetings as her very own play production in which she was the lead actress. She knew her part very well, her mother's, too. Though each year offered a new teacher to interact with, the story never changed. Year after year, Sandy knew what was going to happen from beginning to end.

In the First Act, Sandy would wait for her mother to pull the car out of the dirt floor garage. Sandy would let the dust settle before getting inside to join her mother, a rare treat since Mrs. Stockings never drove. The ride was inevitably utterly silent. Sandy only needed to portray the scared or nervous Daughter, depending on how alert Mrs. Stockings was for playing the role of Mother in any given year.

Act Two would begin as the two players were introduced to the third actor or actress playing the role of Teacher. Sandy and her mother would sit in the cold plastic chairs pulled in front of the teacher's desk, waiting for the opening monologue about what a poor student Sandy had been. Sandy found this to be the least convincing part of the play. Mrs. Stockings would ask why she wasn't informed earlier; the teacher would reply that he or she had sent notes home.

Chapter Three

Sandy would cringe and act as though she was very sorry. And then the teacher would say his or her next line, "I don't know what to do. I've added up all the quizzes and the homework, and she doesn't have the grades to pass."

Mrs. Stockings' cue came next: "Is there any extra credit she could do?"

The teacher would straighten up, trying very hard not to look Sandy in the eye, and pronounce dramatically, "There's been a *lot* of extra credit, but she didn't turn *any* of it in!"

Again, Sandy would feign shame, and one year she even managed a tear. Then everyone fell silent.

The teacher would finally sigh and offer, "The only way she will be able to pass this grade is if she gets an A on the last test."

Mrs. Stockings would then glance down to Sandy, and Sandy would gaze up to her mother. With the same knowing look, mother and daughter would turn to address the teacher. Mrs. Stockings would lightly clear her throat to speak, and when she did her eyes would become like flames. "If my daughter is doing as bad as you say she is, maybe I should go ahead and hold her back another year. That way you'll have the chance to actually *teach* her something." Mrs. Stockings could deliver her lines with an icy chill that would make any teacher squirm.

Then, like clockwork, Act Two would end abruptly, with the teacher's hurried, "Let's see how she does on that last test, thanks for coming in, and let me show you to the door."

Act Three occurred several days later when Sandy took the final test without studying or knowing any of the answers; she didn't even bother to fill in every question. Days would pass, and school would finally let out for summer. Report cards would come in the mail, and Mrs. Stockings would see that, like every year since her husband had died, her daughter had earned straight D's as a result of the perfect score she achieved on her final test. So she could proceed to the next grade without actually ever learning anything.

Sitting in the drama closet, Sandy replayed these past events in her head, rocking from side to side in time with the sound of the clock on the wall, "ticking" to the right, and "tocking" to the left. She rocked until she got dizzy, and then sat down on one of the boxes overflowing with wigs and shirts, the first time she had moved from the place she had stood in since Ms. Bridgewater left the room.

Suddenly, she snapped to attention. She'd been feeling so bad for the last few hours that she'd nearly forgotten the book wrapped in a sweater in her backpack. That morning, she'd been running late, as she almost always was, having slept late and then wrestled through piles of dirty clothes, trying to find the least dirty stuff to wear to school.

As she'd sped through the living room, she nearly forgot the book under the couch cushions until she was halfway out the door. She rushed back in, and in one motion threw the cushion up into the air and grabbed her treasure, nestling it into the red sweater in her schoolbag on her way out the door.

In the fluorescent light of the drama closet, she pulled the book from her bag and stared for a long time. It was by far the strangest book that Sandy had ever seen. The cover was made out of smooth leather, even smoother than the inside heel of her cowboy boots from Tom. She felt terrible for having stuffed it

Chapter Three

under the raggedy cushion of their filthy couch all night. This precious book spent the night next to three quarters, a broken pencil with a chewed off eraser, and a full buffet of stale potato chip crumbs.

The book was like none she'd ever seen before, bound with gold thread and stitched by hand, with stiff pages that felt like glazed fabric. She riffled the pages and marveled at the words and drawings dancing across the pages. She was surprised to see that it was all printed and drawn by hand, not a printer. It reminded her of an ancient war relic she'd seen a picture of in her history textbook.

She opened the first page and saw, in the same elaborate handwriting, the words:

FOR ASHER

Beneath this dedication was a simple portrait of a bumblebee in flight. She flipped the next few pages carefully until she arrived at the heading,

THREE B'S FOR A WANNA BE

For Asher

Chapter One

I'm taking you, dearest friends, to an extra special spot. Hopefully you know by now that if a spot is extra special, nobody really knows about it. Most people find themselves at the end of their lives before they even realize they've never been to this place where I am about to take you. In fact, anyone can go there, at any time, but few answer the call.

I'm going to need you to concentrate, but more importantly enjoy our entire journey. The path that leads to the magical place is as important as the spot itself. So, let's get started.

Begin by putting your mind in a quiet place. I want you to imagine yourself

SINKING INTO THE DEEPEST, SOFTEST DARKNESS YOU CAN THINK OF. IT'S NOT FRIGHTENING. YOU'LL FIND YOURSELF STILL SURROUNDED BY LIGHT AS YOU SLOWLY RELAX INTO THESE PEACEFUL SHADOWS.

When you feel yourself sunk deeply into the comforting darkness, slowly open your mind's eye into a beautiful forest. See the sun sparkling and dancing through brilliant green leaves. Feel a gentle wind rushing through the limbs above you. Smell the rich, damp earth in this mystical chamber of the unknown.

Allow yourself to go a step deeper into this world.

Crouch down in the darkness.

Reach out your hand, and touch the bark of a tree, slick with mist.

Spin slowly, then faster, as the sun disappears and the cool night air surrounds you. Nothing feels darker than the woods

AT NIGHT, BUT YOU CAN SEE THE LIGHT OF THE MOON, THE STARS, THE DISTANT GLOW OF HOUSES.

LISTEN. DO YOU HEAR HIM?

LISTEN FOR A SMOOTH, LOW-PITCHED HUM IN THE DISTANCE, A HISS WRAPPING ITSELF AROUND A TRAIN OF Z'S.

MY FRIEND ASHER PREFERS THE SIMPLE DESCRIPTION: "BUZZ."

THERE'S NOT A WHOLE HIVE OF "BUZZ," ONLY THIS SINGULAR SOUND. THE DARKNESS WHERE YOUR IMAGINATION HAS TAKEN YOU IS THE SAME DARKNESS WHERE I, TOO, FIRST HEARD THIS SOLITARY BUZZ. ON THIS SPOT, READER, I MET AND BEFRIENDED A BUMBLEBEE CALLED ASHER.

THIS IS HIS STORY, BUT ALSO MINE. THIS WAS HOW I CAME TO UNDERSTAND THE LESSON OF THE THREE B'S THAT I WILL SHARE WITH YOU NOW.

Chapter Three

Okay, Sandy thought, looking up at the clock. This is really weird. Is this poetry or something? Why in the world had her mother not wanted her to get her hands on some crazy old book about buzzing bees?

Disappointed, she started to put the book back into her bag when her mind suddenly flashed on a clear memory of her father, sitting by her bed at night, waving the stuffed bee up and down and around, gently "stinging" her face and arms and tummy, saying, "Bee happy, little one. Bee brave. Who do you want to *bee*, little girl? What are you gonna bee? Queen bee?" Sandy could remember dissolving into helpless giggles until he wrapped her up in his arms and hugged her tightly. She felt again how safe and happy she'd been, and then just as quickly realized she'd never have that feeling again.

She felt tears springing to her eyes, and she swallowed hard. She wouldn't think about this now. She'd try never to think of it again. The last thing she needed was for someone to open that door and see her crying. She sniffed loudly and looked back down at the book.

I MET ASHER LATE ONE NIGHT AS I WAS WALKING THROUGH THESE WOODS. I HEARD HIM BUZZING ALONG BY HIMSELF, JUST BEHIND MY LEFT SHOULDER, SHADOWING ME. I DIDN'T KNOW THE FOREST VERY WELL, AND DECIDED TO ASK THE BEE EXACTLY WHERE I WAS.

ASHER INTRODUCED HIMSELF AND SEEMED VERY EAGER TO TALK. IT TURNED OUT THAT HE WAS A VERY WISE BEE...AND AN EXCELLENT CONVERSATIONALIST.

I CAN'T SAY HOW EXACTLY I KNEW, BUT I IMMEDIATELY FELT AN INSTANT RESPECT FOR THE SOLITARY LITTLE BUZZER. WE TALKED LIKE OLD FRIENDS, AND ASHER EXPLAINED THE BEST ROUTES THROUGH THE WOODLAND USING COMMON MARKERS SUCH AS BOULDERS, STREAMS, AND BERRY BUSHES.

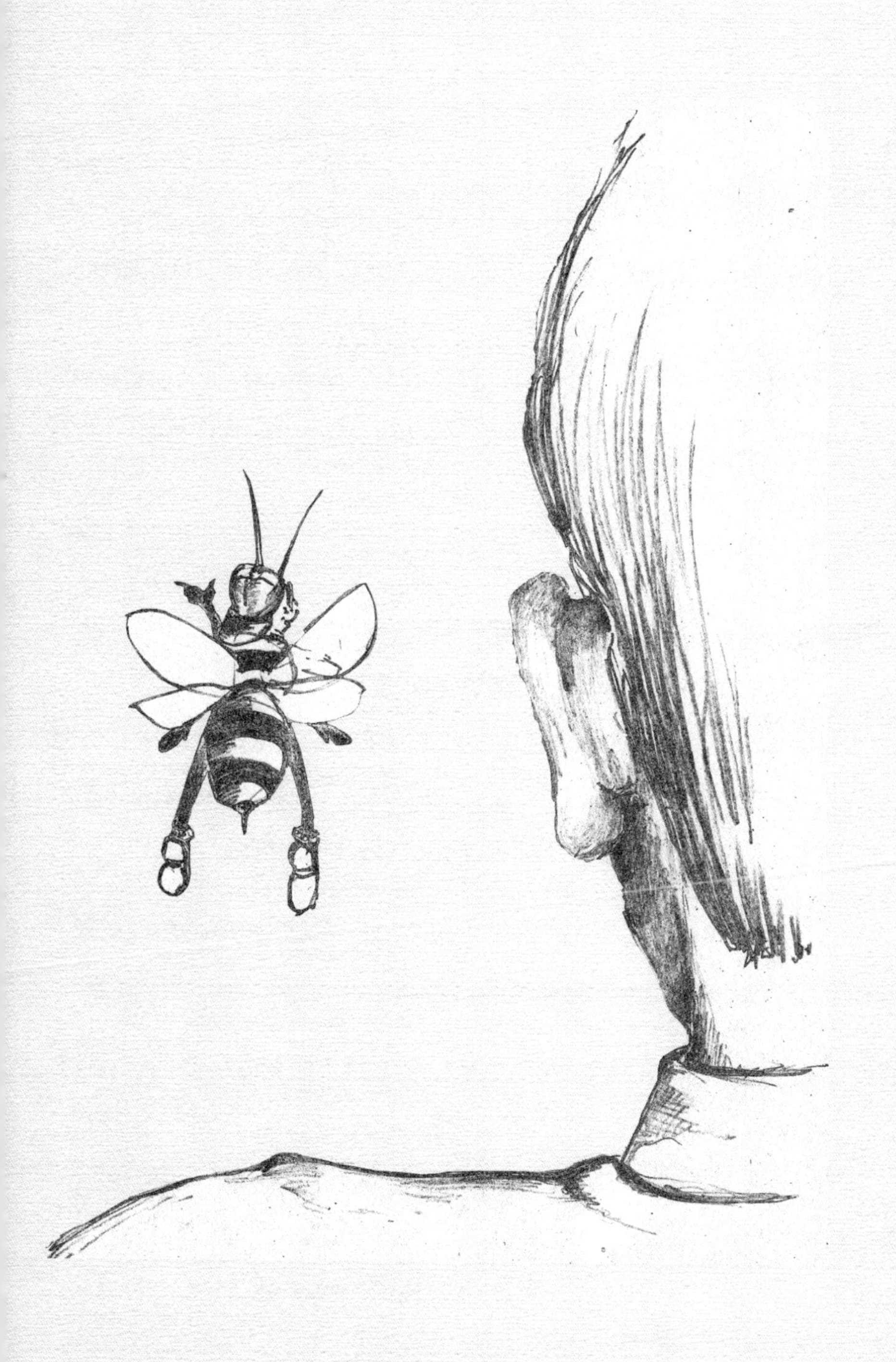

HE SEEMED TO KNOW EVERY NOOK AND CRANNY IN THE FOREST, BUT HE WAS ALSO EAGER TO LEARN NEW THINGS. HE PERCHED ON MY SHOULDER AND DIRECTED ME TO A CLEARING WHERE I SHOWED HIM THE NORTH STAR IN RELATION TO THE BIG DIPPER.

"THIS REMINDS ME OF THE FIRST TIME AN ELDER BEE SHOWED ME AROUND THE FOREST," ASHER SAID. "HE TOLD ME THAT MOSS ONLY GROWS ON THE NORTH SIDE OF A TREE TRUNK, AND THAT LITTLE BIT OF INFORMATION HAS HELPED ME THROUGH MANY WANDERING NIGHTS."

"ANY PARTICULAR REASON FOR YOUR WANDERING?" I ASKED CURIOUSLY.

"WELL, I HAVE ALWAYS LIKED TO WANDER JUST FOR THE SAKE OF WANDERING, IT'S TRUE, BUT IT'S MOSTLY SOMETHING I PICKED UP WHEN I

WAS, AHEM, THE WORST BEE IN MY HIVE."

HOW, YOU MAY WONDER, CAN A BEE BE BOTH WISE AND THE WORST BEE IN HIS HIVE?

WELL, YOU HAVE TO UNDERSTAND, AS ASHER TAUGHT ME, THE INNER WORKINGS OF A BEE HIVE. IT ALL CENTERS ON INSTINCT.

YOU CAN'T TEACH INSTINCTS. YOU EITHER HAVE THEM OR YOU DON'T, AND BEFORE ASHER CAME ALONG, HIS HIVE BELIEVED THAT WORKER BEES LIKE HIM WERE BORN WITH ONLY THREE BASIC INSTINCTS: TO COLLECT POLLEN FROM FLOWERS, TO PRODUCE HONEY, AND TO BUILD AND PROTECT THE HIVE.

THE BEES IN ASHER'S HIVE BELIEVED THAT THEY COULD DETERMINE WHERE EACH BEE SHOULD RANK IN THE HIVE BASED ON THEIR INSTINCTIVE

ABILITIES AT BIRTH. SOME BEES WERE BORN WITH STRONG INSTINCTS – THEY COLLECTED POLLEN, PRODUCED HONEY, AND BUILT BETTER THAN OTHERS. THESE FORTUNATE YOUNGSTERS WOULD GROW UP TO HAVE A HIGHER RANK IN THE HIVE THAN THOSE BEES WHOSE INITIAL INSTINCTS WERE NOT AS STRONG OR AS OBVIOUS.

THE HIGH-RANKING BEES RAN THE BEE MEETINGS, AND WERE ALLOWED CERTAIN PRIVILEGES AND THE BEST OF EVERYTHING THE HIVE HAD TO OFFER. ALL BEES WERE EXPECTED TO ACCEPT THEIR POSITION AND LIVE THEIR LIFE ACCORDINGLY, SO THEY DID.

BEING INCREDIBLY PROUD CREATURES, IT WENT AGAINST THEIR BEE NATURE TO TALK ABOUT THE TROUBLES THEY WERE HAVING, AND THEY NEVER DISCUSSED HOW THEY MIGHT BETTER THEMSELVES. DON'T GET ME WRONG. TALKING ABOUT THEIR PROBLEMS WASN'T ILLEGAL, JUST FROWNED UPON. NOBODY EVEN THOUGHT TO DO IT BECAUSE THEY'D BEEN BROUGHT UP TO BELIEVE THAT THEY HAD TO ACCEPT WHAT THEY WERE GIVEN WITHOUT HOPE OF IMPROVING.

THEN ALONG CAME ASHER. SOMEHOW, ASHER WAS BORN WITH CLOSE TO NO BEE INSTINCT. HE WAS TINY, TOO, AND TALKATIVE, AND BECAUSE HE WAS SO DIFFERENT FROM THE OTHER BEES, AND MADE SO MANY MISTAKES, THE OTHER BEES FELT A LITTLE BETTER ABOUT THEIR OWN PROBLEMS WHEN THEY MADE FUN OF ASHER.

HIS INCREDIBLY FOUL-SMELLING HONEY WAS THE STUFF OF LEGEND AT HIVE PARTIES.

HE GATHERED THE LEAST AMOUNT OF POLLEN FROM THE FIELDS OF ANY OF THE BEES, AND NEVER BROUGHT ANY HOME FROM THE HIGHEST QUALITY FLOWERS. "HE'S NEAR-SIGHTED BUT THAT SHOULDN'T MATTER," THE OTHER BEES WOULD SAY, "SO HE MUST JUST BE DUMB."

HE FLEW OFF BY HIMSELF WHENEVER HE COULD AND DID WHO KNOWS WHAT, THE OTHER BEES WOULD ROLL THEIR EYES.

HE NEVER PAID ATTENTION TO WHERE HE WAS GOING, AND HE WAS NEAR-SIGHTED, LIKE THEY SAID, SO HE WOULD INEVITABLY BUMP INTO THINGS OR GET LOST. PRODUCTION WAS FORCED TO STOP ON SEVERAL OCCASIONS WHILE THE HIVE SENT RELUCTANT SEARCH PARTIES TO FIND HIM.

His hive mates knew he was born that way, and didn't bother trying to help him but instead just ignored him. Some worked hard to exclude him, just in case some of his strange ways might rub off on them. No one would be caught dead hanging out with him, so Asher didn't have any friends.

He escaped in the nights to fly by himself because somehow he felt less alone when he was by himself than he did when he was surrounded by others.

Chapter Three

Sandy looked up from the book and sighed. She felt again like she might cry. Could she ever relate to this pathetic loner of a bee! She closed the book for a minute and stared at the door of the costume room. Where in the world had her mother gotten this book? Why didn't she want anyone to see it, or even look at it herself?

She sat for a very long time, lost in her thoughts. When she finally looked up, the clock said 4:40, and she had still done none of the work Mrs. Bridgewater asked. "I guess I just don't have good hive cleaning instincts," she smirked to herself.

Sandy looked listlessly around the drama closet, but then perked up a little. She noticed that the clothes were arranged in a pattern, instead of the cluttered mess she had thought they were. She was just about to stand up and investigate further when the office door opened, and Ms. Bridgewater walked in. Her jaw was tight, and her hands were clenched so tightly that her knuckles were turning white.

As she watched Ms. Bridgewater's eyes dart around the room, Sandy was curious. "I'm not surprised that she's mad," Sandy thought. "I know doing nothing was wrong. But why does she seem so shocked that I didn't do the work? Didn't she tell me my 'reputation preceded' me?"

Slowly, it dawned on Sandy that, for the first time in a very long time, someone had actually expected something more from her, and she didn't deliver. Ms. Bridgewater was disappointed in her.

When Ms. Bridgewater opened her mouth to speak, Sandy readied herself for the expected lecture. But none came. Instead, a smooth, controlled voice said, "Very well, Sandy, I will see you here at three o'clock tomorrow. You are free to go." And before waiting for a response, Ms. Bridgewater walked gracefully out the door, her head held high.

Sandy was stunned. She took another look around the room, then walked out into the open hallway, noticing that the smell of the drama closet followed her, lingering in the sixth grade hall when she was at her locker, in the parking lot as she walked beside the flagpole, and on the trail through the woods where she used to run free.

She was tempted to stop and look for a bee hive, to see if she could see any little bees who might talk to her, but then she felt stupid and continued home. "You can't do dumb baby stuff like that anymore," she told herself. "You're in sixth grade now, and you need to act like it. It's a rough world, especially for you: you know you're not smart, and you're definitely not lucky, and no one likes you, so you need to stay tough, not let your guard down and get lost in dumb fantasies."

As she walked up the broken concrete steps into her house, she stopped to sit a minute. She didn't want to deal with her sad mother yet, and for some reason she wasn't quite ready to sneak this crazy book back into its velvet bag. Something about it brought up thoughts and feelings that just barely rose to the surface for a quick appearance and then darted away again. This disturbed Sandy and intrigued her at the same time.

The steps were as wide as Sandy was long, making them perfect for stretching out for a nap on any warm day. There were only three of them, but they were all hers.

She sat on her steps until the sun went down, and her mother came out to look for her. Mrs. Stockings stood in the door watching Sandy, then opened the screen lightly and crouched down on the upper-most step as though she was on the edge of a pond. She wrapped her long, thin arms around her daughter's chest, and Sandy closed her eyes and nestled her cheek into her mother's soft, chestnut-colored hair. This wasn't the first time her mother had hugged her, but it had been a long, long time.

After a moment, Mrs. Stockings sat back with a puzzled look on her face and said, "You smell like the theater."

Chapter Four

"I'm dead!" sulked Sandy, rolling lazily out of bed the next day. She had gotten up late again. Although she wasn't sorry to be missing class, showing up late meant all the attention would be focused on her. She hated her classmate's eyes scrutinizing her as she walked through the door. Plus, her teachers always stopped their lessons and stared at her until she took her seat. Sandy didn't know why they didn't just shine a spot light on her so that everyone could have a clear view of who was disturbing class time.

Waking up wasn't even the trickiest part about being on time. For Sandy, scavenging the floor looking for relatively clean clothes to wear was much more time-consuming. She'd spent this particular morning trying to get a jelly stain out of Kyle's (third son) camouflage pants so she could wear them to school. They showed the least amount of dirt, after all.

The battle continued for another half hour as she looked for an almost-clean shirt to match. The only thing she could find was one of Clyde's black t-shirts. Sandy had never worn this particular one before, and she threw it over her head, trying hard not to breathe in the gross smell.

The bell rang for lunch just as she was walking along the sidewalk beside the playground. Three hundred kids poured out of the main building to sit outside and enjoy their break. Several sixth graders hurried for the smallest and most out-of-the-way corners of the courtyard. Those not fortunate enough to have a place saved for them with a group of friends were forced to sit in the sun along the chain link fence that bordered the school's playground and courtyards. Not only was the fence uncomfortable to sit against, but these seats were also in plain view of the eighth graders eating their lunches on the grassy courtyards.

Sandy, not having the luxury of a friendly clique, was always found directly across from the courtyard, and therefore presented a "bull's-eye" for the eighth graders. In the two weeks she had been in sixth grade, she had been the target of empty soda cans, three bruised apples, and a handful of pennies. The objects were hurled from the middle of various groups, and Sandy could never see exactly who threw what.

Lunchtime was the worst time for any student without a friend. The teachers turned a blind eye when it came to the goings-on in the courtyard. They huddled around the picnic tables next to the door and talked amongst themselves. Sandy snorted a little, thinking they might be the most exclusive of all the cliques out here.

Sandy took a seat against the fence, only then remembering that she hadn't packed anything to eat. She sighed and decided to

Chapter Four

read more about Asher. For reasons she could not fully explain, she had decided not to put the book back in the velvet bag last night. Partly it was because it would have been hard to do. Her mother actually fixed Sandy dinner for a change–spaghetti and a jar of sauce, but that was a real treat these days–and then they sat together, looking through her mother's things for awhile before her mother said, "I can hardly believe it, but I'm a little bored with myself, Sandy!" Mrs. Stockings laughed a small, tired laugh, and added, "Wanna see if there's something good on TV?"

Sandy had jumped up and rushed to find the remote for their little television before her mother could change her mind and head up to bed. They watched an old movie until they both fell asleep, snuggled together on the couch. Later, somehow Sandy had made it up to her bed, too sleepy to think about the book, and then was in too big of a rush that morning to put the book back, anyway.

In the far less cozy environment of the schoolyard, she pulled it from where it was nestled again in her backpack and flipped until she found where she'd stopped the day before in the drama closet.

Because Asher was told so often that he was destined to fail, he believed it. He did little to change anything. He wasn't completely miserable, but he definitely knew he wasn't happy. He just didn't know what to do about it and wondered if maybe some bees are just destined to be unhappy.

A nagging intuition that this wasn't true, a small buzzing feeling he'd get whenever he would think that he was just a loser in life, kept him flying at night. On one of these night flights, Asher felt that he'd had enough of feeling so empty. He was suddenly determined to be more.

"I bet I could be a great worker bee," Asher thought, and before he could stop himself, he said aloud, "I know that I can

BE THE BEST BEE IN MY HIVE!" HE LAUGHED A LAUGH THAT ECHOED THROUGHOUT THE QUIET FOREST. AS SOON AS HE'D SAID IT, HE KNEW IT WAS TRUE, BUT HE LOOKED AROUND, EMBARRASSED, TO SEE IF ANYONE HAD HEARD HIM.

HE FLEW ON, DECIDING THEN AND THERE TO DO WHATEVER IT TOOK TO MAKE THIS HAPPEN, TO LEARN HOW TO BE THE BEST BEE AND THEN TO BE THE BEST.

BUT THE VERY NEXT DAY, ASHER WOKE UP WITH SOME DOUBT. "I DON'T KNOW WHERE TO BEGIN," HE THOUGHT. "I DON'T EVEN KNOW WHAT BEING THE BEST WORKER BEE LOOKS LIKE." TRYING NOT TO GET DISCOURAGED, HE PONDERED THIS PROBLEM AND SUDDENLY A NAME CAME TO MIND: "FELIX," HE SAID ALOUD. "HE'S BEEN A WORKER BEE FOR MANY YEARS. I'LL SEE IF I CAN FOLLOW HIM AROUND AND LEARN ALL THAT HE KNOWS!"

DESPITE HOW EASY THIS SOLUTION SEEMED, ASHER HAD HIS DOUBTS. HIS SMALL SIZE AND HISTORY OF MISTAKES AND MISHAPS HAD MADE HIM VERY UNPOPULAR IN THE HIVE. WHAT'S MORE, NO ONE EVER ASKED FOR HELP - AT LEAST ASHER HAD NEVER HEARD OF ANYONE ASKING FOR HELP BEFORE - AND NEITHER HAD FELIX, WHO WAS VERY SURPRISED AT ASHER'S REQUEST.

"THE REST OF US JUST KNOW HOW TO DO IT, ASHER. IT'S CALLED INSTINCT. YOU AIN'T GOT IT. WE DO. PRETTY SIMPLE."

"I UNDERSTAND THAT, FELIX, BUT I JUST WANT TO WATCH YOU COLLECT POLLEN FOR ONE DAY. I JUST WANT TO SEE HOW YOU DO IT. I BELIEVE IT WILL HELP ME GET BETTER AT IT MYSELF. I WON'T BE A BOTHER. YOU WON'T EVEN KNOW I'M HERE."

FELIX KNEW ASHER'S REPUTATION AND THAT HE WAS BY FAR THE WORST BEE IN THE HIVE, SO HE COULDN'T UNDERSTAND WHY ASHER WOULD WANT TO FOLLOW HIM AROUND, WATCHING HIM COLLECT POLLEN. HE DIDN'T THINK IT WOULD MAKE A BIT OF DIFFERENCE, BUT AT LAST HE RELENTED.. "IT'S FINE BY ME," FELIX HUFFED. "BUT DON'T GET YOUR HOPES UP. YOU WEREN'T BORN TO WORK WELL."

ASHER THANKED FELIX PROFUSELY AND FOLLOWED HIM TO WORK. IT TURNED OUT TO BE THE HARDEST DAY OF ASHER'S YOUNG LIFE, ESPECIALLY WHEN HE TRIED TO DO WHAT FELIX DID. AT FIRST IT JUST DIDN'T FEEL RIGHT, BUT WHEN HE RELAXED AND FORGOT ALL ABOUT ALL THE BEES WHO BELIEVED HE COULDN'T DO IT, HE FOUND HIMSELF PICKING THINGS UP QUICKER THAN HE'D EVER THOUGHT HE COULD.

HE ASKED TWO THOUSAND QUESTIONS, AND BECAME FASCINATED WITH THE SAME JOB THAT HAD BORED HIM EVERY DAY SINCE HE COULD REMEMBER. EVEN TOUGH OLD FELIX MARVELED AT THE QUICK CHANGE A LITTLE ATTENTION MADE IN ASHER, EVEN GROWING TO RESPECT THIS FUNNY KID AND HIS ABILITIES.

"I GOTTA HAND IT TO YOU, KID," FELIX SAID QUIETLY AT THE END OF THE WEEK. "YOU'VE REALLY GOT WHAT IT TAKES. WHERE'VE YOU BEEN HIDING ALL THAT TALENT, HUH?"

ASHER JUST SMILED AND FLEW OFF TO ASK ANOTHER HIGH-PRODUCER IN THE HIVE IF HE COULD DO THE SAME THING: FOLLOW HIM AROUND AND LEARN FROM HIM THE SKILLS AND TECHNIQUES THAT MADE HIM A GREAT POLLEN GATHERER.

For six solid weeks, Asher flew through the hive asking anyone he could find if he could watch how they worked. He quickly saw that no two bees were alike, and Asher tried to learn from the skills and abilities of each one in the hive.

A problem arose, though: nobody could understand how the worst bee in the hive had begun to produce the best honey in half the time it took the highest-ranked worker. They rechecked his records and birth charts, and couldn't believe that he was the same bee.

After many more months, while Asher continued improving, all the bees got together for a meeting to discuss the strange case. Many of them admired his

WORK, BUT AS MANY WERE FRIGHTENED AND DISAPPROVING BECAUSE THEY COULDN'T UNDERSTAND HOW HE HAD MANAGED TO BECOME DIFFERENT THAN WHAT THEY HAD ALWAYS BEEN.

BARRY, THE HIGHEST-RANKED BEE BEFORE ASHER'S IMPROVEMENT, CALLED THE MEETING TO ORDER AND BROUGHT ASHER FORWARD TO ADDRESS THE WHOLE HIVE. "WHAT HAVE YOU DONE TO YOURSELF, ASHER, TO DEFEAT YOUR DESTINY AS THE WORST BEE IN THE HIVE?" BARRY ASKED.

Asher stood confidently in front of the colony. "You all know that I followed the best of you around for weeks, acquiring new skills as I learned from your great abilities. I wasn't born like you, with the same instincts, but now I know that doesn't mean being the worst was my *destiny*. I believed that for years, too, but if you believe in yourself, instead of in what everyone tells you about yourself, well, the results in my case speak for themselves!" Asher laughed but noticed that many of the bees still looked skeptical. They seemed unable to make the connection between the way Asher had closely observed their work methods and then improved his own abilities. As far as they were concerned, it was just easier to

BELIEVE THAT HE WAS AN ENTIRELY DIFFERENT BEE. AND THAT COULDN'T BE A GOOD THING.

A LOUD MURMUR WENT THROUGH THE ENTIRE ASSEMBLY. THE BEES IN ASHER'S HIVE SIMPLY DIDN'T UNDERSTAND HIS SUGGESTION THAT LEARNING COULD OVERCOME INSTINCT, AND BECAUSE THEY DIDN'T UNDERSTAND, THEY WERE FEARFUL AND QUICKLY GREW HOSTILE.

"SUDDENLY HE'S SUPERIOR TO US? HE'S ATTACKING OUR BIRTH GIFTS!" SOME SHOUTED.

"HE'S SAYING WE'RE WORTHLESS. WHO DOES HE THINK HE IS?" YELLED OTHERS.

"LET'S THROW HIM OUT OF THE HIVE," MANY AGREED. "WE SHOULD'VE DONE IT YEARS AGO."

HEAD WORKER BEE BARRY WAS KIND AND BRAVE, A LITTLE MORE ENLIGHTENED THAN THE REST,

AND HE MANAGED TO CALM THE GREAT BUZZ. "ASHER'S SUCCESS CAME FROM HIS HARD WORK, FROM HIS BELIEF THAT HE COULD BE SOMETHING MORE THAN WE'D ALWAYS TOLD HIM HE WAS," BARRY BEGAN. "TO ME, THAT'S IMPRESSIVE. HIS ACCOMPLISHMENTS DON'T LESSEN OUR OWN."

AT THE RISK OF HAVING THE WHOLE ASSEMBLED HIVE TURN ON HIM, BARRY CONTINUED. "ASHER'S SIMPLY THE BEST WORKER BEE IN THE HIVE NOW. THAT'S WHAT I KNOW AND ALL I NEED TO KNOW. I AM WILLING TO STEP DOWN FROM MY POSITION AND RELINQUISH MY TITLE TO HIM."

THOUGH ASHER WAS TOUCHED BY THE GESTURE, AND GRATEFUL TO BARRY FOR SAVING HIS FUZZY HIDE FROM THE NOW CALMING MOB, HE DIDN'T FEEL HE NEEDED THE HEAD WORKER BEE TITLE. JUST KNOWING HE WAS THE BEST SATISFIED HIM.

"I'M READY TO HELP THE REST OF THESE BEES, THOUGH," HE TOLD HIS FRIEND BARRY. "LET'S WORK TOGETHER TO TEACH ALL THE BEES WHAT I HAVE LEARNED, SO THAT EVERYONE CAN BE HAPPY AND PRODUCTIVE, THE VERY BEST BEE THEY CAN BE. I CALL MY METHOD 'THREE B'S FOR A WANNABE.' GET IT? BECOME, BE NEAR, AND BE READY. I CAN TEACH IT TO EVERYONE, AND THEN THEY'LL SEE THAT, EVEN THOUGH IT'S HARD WORK, IT'S SOMETHING EVERYONE CAN DO."

"THAT'S A GREAT IDEA, ASHER," BARRY SAID.

Chapter Four

Time had flown for Sandy while she read. She looked up from the book and around at the courtyard without really seeing what was in front of her, lost as she was in the story. "It's not really as weird as I thought it was before," she mused. "I actually really like it, and I can definitely relate in some ways to Asher before he learns how to be a better bee...but I don't see how Asher's story could really apply to me. Instincts aren't my problem. Except maybe my instinct to pound Clyde's ugly face in," she smirked.

As if on cue, suddenly, a sharp pain seared through her forehead, right between her eyes, and knocked her back slightly. Sandy noticed an acorn rolling around the gravel beneath her, and moved her hand up to feel the lump immediately springing from where she had been hit. The sharp pain shifted into a dull throbbing and made her vision blur for a second.

She shook her head to clear her vision and saw, standing barely ten yards away, Clyde Debrah and two of his moronic friends, Bud and Bret, laughing and slapping hands. Sandy flew to her feet, but not before scooping up three half-dollar-sized rocks.

Clyde sauntered up to her, still chuckling to himself, followed by his two henchmen. "Thought you might like another nut t'go with that collection you've got at home. Maybe it could keep your mama company," Clyde laughed, signaling his friends to do the same.

"You miserable... I... I can't believe that... Oooh!" was all Sandy could manage to say, still slightly dazed by the blow. While she stuttered and stumbled furiously, Clyde noticed something that made him angrier than any insult Sandy could have come up with.

"My shirt!" he snarled. "That's my favorite black shirt! Where did you get that, Sock-Stinks?"

Sandy smiled. Despite the disgust she felt with herself for having stooped to wearing Clyde's hand-me-down, his reaction made it worth it. She felt suddenly inspired: "Is this *your* shirt, Deb-rah? I had no *idea*. I almost didn't wear it today because I thought it was so *girly*," Sandy said, pulling the hem out in front of her and looking contemptuously first at the shirt and then at Clyde.

Bud and Bret laughed a little, so Clyde was beside himself with rage. He rushed toward Sandy before his friends could grab him, and began tearing at her schoolbag. She screamed, and hit him on the back with her free hand, but she was too small to do any damage by herself.

"Fair's fair, Spotty! You stole my shirt, now I get something of yours."

"Oh! Clyde, you can have your stupid shirt back! Leave my things alone!" Sandy screamed, forgetting where she was.

"I don't want it back! You've contaminated it. Besides, I think this might be a good lesson for you." As Clyde said this, he threw the bag down, his right hand clutching the leather book. "What have we got here? I didn't know you knew how to read, Sock-Stinks."

"Give it back, Clyde! I'm serious," Sandy growled, giving up trying to use physical force and hoping against hope that she might scare him.

"Oh, you're serious, are you? Did you hear that guys, lil' San-dee is sewious," Clyde said in his infamous baby voice. A small crowd had gathered, growing bigger by the minute, most of them laughing at Clyde's antics.

"Give it back, *now*!" Sandy growled, so firmly that Clyde stopped laughing, and took a small step back. But then he looked around, saw the crowd was in his favor, and regained his composure.

"Or else what?" Clyde mocked.

Sandy, however, was not in the mood to try using reason to get what she wanted. In her opinion, she had given him his chance. Shifting one of the rocks into her right hand, Sandy drew back and hurled it as fast and hard as any boy ever could. Before Clyde could detect any sign of danger, the rock smashed against his wrist, causing him to drop the book to the ground. Clyde opened his mouth as though to let out a lion's roar, but no sound came out. The crowd huddled tighter to get a better look at this new turn of events.

Sandy wasted no time waiting for retaliation; she scrambled forward and grabbed the book before Clyde had opened his eyes. With the book in her hand, Sandy tried to break through the wall of onlookers, but her efforts were wasted. She was trapped inside a circle of peers hungry for a fight.

When she turned around, Sandy saw that Clyde had gotten over the initial shock of the blow, and was moving forward to attack. In another fluid movement, Sandy slipped the second rock into her throwing hand, and reared back to strike again. Clyde stopped.

"What're you going to do with that?" Clyde asked, trying to buy time.

"Don't come any closer, Deb-rah, or you'll find out."

"I want my shirt back!" Clyde screamed, sounding more like an infant than a bully.

"I said you could have your stupid shirt back! I don't even like it, but you'll have to wait until tomorrow to get it." Sandy decided that she didn't really want to hit Clyde again, and weighed the chances that she might still be able to talk her way out of serious trouble. A few chants from the crowd, however, told Sandy that Clyde would never back down to a sixth grade girl under the eyes of thirty eighth grade boys.

She clutched the rock even tighter in her hand, still cocked and ready to fire. Clyde didn't say anything. He kept looking around at the people, and seemed to indicate something to his henchman with his eyes. Suddenly Bud and Bret jumped out of the bystanders and rushed forward, grabbing at her arms.

She scrambled away from them, and then ducked just in time to see Clyde running full speed in her direction. As she backed up, she managed to aim the rock in his direction, but as she threw it, a hand reached out from the crowd and knocked her arm. The rock sailed over the heads of the circle, parting them as it went, and headed for the front of the main building.

Everyone turned to see the stone descend. To Sandy's horror, the rock sped into the center picnic table full of teachers and must have landed with a substantial impact, sending a can spraying something out in every direction. The teachers scrambled over each other, trying to escape getting soaked.

The scene was like the battleground in a war movie, with the teachers playing soldiers unexpectedly ambushed. Mrs. Fran, in an attempt to dive from her seat, got her foot caught and flopped down face first onto Ms. Carson's leg, knocking her to the ground. Ms. Slaughter, the gym teacher, dropped backwards and rolled to safety, as though she had been training for just such an attack. Only one teacher remained perfectly still, as if glued to her seat. Sandy couldn't mistake Ms. Bridgewater's grim expression and tightly pinned hair.

A student, panting with laughter, ran up to the crowd surrounding Sandy and Clyde, and screamed, "Something just dropped out of the sky and exploded Bridgewater's drink! There's soda spraying everywhere! And Bridgewater's just sitting there! It's the craziest thing I ever saw!"

Clyde turned toward Sandy with a smirk stretched clear across his face, "You're *dead*, Sock-Stinks."

Chapter Five

Life can be very stingy about who gets holes to crawl in and when. Sandy never seemed to have enough holes. Right then, she felt so small she could have crawled under a seashell. The bell rang for class to start, and all three hundred children poured back through the doors of the main building. Sandy stayed behind to think. She wouldn't have been so nervous if she had any other subject to go to, but she had math next. Sandy had no idea what Ms. Bridgewater might be capable of.

She could hear the warning bell sound, so she started to walk toward the building. She passed by the picnic table, still dripping wet, and felt her legs go stiff. Everything inside of her told her to run away, but she couldn't. "I'll imagine myself in a deep, dark forest," she said to herself. "Maybe I can hang out with Asher, and maybe he'll teach me how to quit messing up so much."

Sandy was the last student to enter the room. She walked

through the door as the bell rang to start class. Ms. Bridgewater was sitting quietly at her desk, reading over some papers and marking them with a pen every now and then. Sandy expected to be called over to her desk, but Ms. Bridgewater didn't even look up. Sandy let out a deep sigh of relief. Clyde hadn't gotten the chance to tell on her yet.

She made her way to her seat in the back of the class on the right side of the room, next to the window. Even though Ms. Bridgewater didn't officially assign seats, by the third day of class everyone knew who was going to sit where. As she got closer to her seat, however, Sandy felt the blood rush out of her face. A rock sat on the top of her desk. But it wasn't just any rock; it was *her* rock, still dripping with diet soda. She slunk down into her chair and tried to will a giant hole to open up and swallow her.

Ms. Bridgewater looked around the room, checking attendance, and then got up from her seat. The students noticed that the upper part of her blouse was completely soaked with cola. Her hair, though still taut and orderly, shone with dampness under the lights. Nothing, however, appeared to be different in her manner. Her steps were still short and agile, her chin raised high, and her back perfectly straight. She stared out at the class, clearing her throat before speaking.

"Huh-hem," she said. "Please, open your books to page thirty-five. We will be reviewing fractions today. You will have a quiz on Thursday on the first two chapters." Her voice was so calm that, apart from her dripping blouse, Ms. Bridgewater appeared to have had a normal lunch break.

Sandy didn't understand. None of her classmates would

have put the rock on her desk. The only person near the rock was Ms. Bridgewater, but her not saying anything made no sense. Sandy watched her teacher carefully. Every once in a while Ms. Bridgewater would catch her eye, but Sandy didn't notice any meaning behind the looks outside the usual "pay attention to the lesson." Sandy was more nervous about what would happen in detention after school than she had ever been about any other punishment she had ever received. Ms. Bridgewater's manner was downright unnerving.

Startled, Sandy jumped in her seat when the bell rang, ending class. School was over, and if Sandy had thought walking to see Ms. Bridgewater in the classroom was hard, nothing prepared her for the anxiety she felt for her one-on-one detention. She stood up from her chair, grabbing her schoolbag, and walked slowly down the aisle. Ms. Bridgewater had returned to her desk and did not look up at Sandy as she passed. But just as Sandy was about to leave the room, she heard her name.

"Ms. Stockings," Ms. Bridgewater said evenly.

Sandy turned around slowly, and saw at last the stern face she had been expecting. She dragged her feet across the floor to her teacher's desk.

"I'm really sorry…" Sandy began.

"Ms. Stockings," Ms. Bridgewater interrupted. "I have been informed that you have in your possession a brown book reported to be stolen. I have also been informed that this missing book might be in your schoolbag. Normally, I do not bother with matters that students should solve among themselves, but I have a very low tolerance for thieves, so I'm sure you can appreciate my present position." Ms. Bridgewater said this as though looking for a response, but Sandy couldn't bring herself to say anything. This whole mess seemed like a very bad dream from which she wasn't allowed to wake up.

Ms. Bridgewater, seeing that Sandy was unable to speak, continued. "I am not, however, going to invade your privacy by force, but would appreciate it if you would turn out the contents of your schoolbag here on the floor in front of me." And then smiling slightly, she added, "That is, unless you know of the book in question and would be so kind as to hand it over."

Sandy didn't know what to do. If Clyde had already told Ms. Bridgewater about the book, then she wouldn't be able to explain that it belonged to her mother. Half an hour ago, Sandy couldn't have imagined more fear than she felt of her teacher, but she couldn't compare that to the terror of her mother finding out the book was lost forever. She felt faint.

"Well?" Ms. Bridgewater said impatiently.

"I don't know," Sandy said, trying to stall for time.

"You don't *know*?" her teacher said, frowning at this unexpected response.

"Well, I do have the book you're talking about, but it doesn't belong to Clyde."

"I never mentioned Mr. De-Bray, Ms. Stockings, but as it turns out he is the student to whom I referred. He has given me a description of the book, and told me you might have it. Show me the book in your bag, and I will see if the two match."

"But it's a set-up, a trick..." Sandy started.

"Now," Ms. Bridgewater stated.

Sandy reluctantly unzipped her bag, and reached in for the book. As she pulled it out, she watched Ms. Bridgewater's expression turn from one of smug satisfaction to a look of absolute horror.

"But—this can't be his!" she gasped, taking the book from Sandy.

"Is it not how he described?" Sandy asked, confused by her teacher's response.

"No, it is exactly as he described it…" Ms. Bridgewater trailed off, staring at the book as though she knew something more than she was saying. Her face, usually the picture of control, now looked bewildered.. She examined the book very closely, turning the pages over one by one, until finally she closed it with a snap that made Sandy jump.

"I am afraid I am going to have to keep this, Ms. Stockings."

"But you said it wasn't Clyde's!" Sandy shrieked.

"Yes, well, there are some unforeseen circumstances, and so I will need to do some further investigation," Ms. Bridgewater said coolly. But as she started again, her voice shook slightly. "I'm not sure what I'm going to do. I… I… I'm simply not sure!"

"But this isn't fair," Sandy said.

"Ms. Stockings, I will join you in my office in a few moments. Please go!"

Sandy picked up her bag and walked out into the hall, feeling her last bit of hope slip away.

Once inside the drama office, Sandy flopped down on top of the box of wigs to wait for her teacher. Before long, she heard the clicking of heels along the tile outside the door.

"I've decided to join you today," Ms. Bridgewater said as

she entered. "It was silly of me to leave you alone here yesterday, and I need to get this office in order for the tryouts."

Maybe she took the book to punish her for the rock throwing, Sandy thought. Maybe if she could convince Ms. Bridgewater of her sincere repentance…"I'm really sorry about the rock, Ms. Bridgewater. I really am. It was an…" Sandy started to say.

"Did your mother give you that book, Sandy?" her teacher asked, interrupting her.

"No, ma'am. I sort of found it," Sandy said looking at the floor.

"Found it where? Does she know you have it?"

"No, ma'am. I was gonna put it back today. I was reading it at lunch before Clyde…and yesterday, actually, when I was supposed to be…"

"Come over here, and help me move this," Ms. Bridgewater said, crossing over to the box of swords and plates. "I need these props cleaned. There is dust on the plates, and some of the swords are stained."

Sandy could see that, indeed, many of the swords had sticky red gunk on the blades.

"Ms. Bridgewater?" Sandy asked, picking up one of the swords to look at.

"Yes?" her teacher responded impatiently, taking the sword from Sandy and putting it back into the box.

"It seemed like you'd seen my book before," Sandy said cautiously.

"Yes?"

"And I was wondering if you might know what it was, or where my mother might have gotten it," Sandy said, looking deep into her teacher's eyes.

Ms. Bridgewater seemed to want to answer but was unable. After a moment's silence, she looked back down to the box and said, "There are cleaning supplies in the hallway. I do not want to speak about the book anymore today."

Sandy sighed, and walked toward the door.

"Ms. Stockings," Ms. Bridgewater said. "I might have left some of the cleaning supplies in my room."

"I'll get them," Sandy said, turning back to the door with another sigh.

"Ms. Stockings," Ms. Bridgewater said again, stopping Sandy again. "I hope that the book will be safe tonight. I left it in the bottom right drawer of my desk. It's the only one that doesn't lock, and I would be very sad to lose it. There would be nothing for me to do if I did… though, things do sometimes get misplaced."

With narrowed her eyes, Sandy stared at her teacher. Ms. Bridgewater's stern face broke into a small smile; she seemed unusually kind, unlike Sandy had ever seen her before.

Sandy didn't know what to say, so she turned and walked out the door, and into the hall. "She's sneaky. She must be trying to trick me," she thought as she walked down the hall. "She'll try and catch me in the act of stealing from her, and then I'll get expelled." Sandy decided to leave the book where it was, but as she crossed the classroom to pick up the bucket in the corner, she remembered her mother, and how upset she would be if she remembered the velvet bag and found it empty. Things had been going better for them, and she was afraid her mother would never speak to her again if the book disappeared forever. Besides, she was actually really enjoying the book and wanted to know what happened, what these Three B's things were…

"I'll have to risk it," Sandy decided. "It was her own fault for telling me where the book was." She walked over to the desk and opened the bottom drawer. The book was sitting on top of a pad of paper and some extra pieces of chalk. She grabbed it and rushed out of the room, toward her locker, forgetting the bucket and cleaning supplies. She felt excited, relieved, and a little guilty.

Then she rounded the corner of the sixth grade hall and ran right into Clyde Debrah, flanked by Bud and Bret.

"Well, well, well, if it isn't little Spotty Sock-Stinks!" he said, pushing Sandy backwards and knocking her to the floor. "Nice job with that rock today, Ugly. You're not trying to get out of detention with Bridgewater are you?"

"Leave me alone, Clyde. I don't want to fight with you. I'm just going to my locker for a second," Sandy said, trying to stand up while hiding the book.

"You're not going anywhere," he said with a laugh. "I don't care if you wanna fight or not. I still owe you one for that rock you threw at my arm. How 'bout you don't fight and make it even easier on me and my boys here, Freckle Butt?"

Sandy felt herself losing her temper, "You started it! You threw an acorn at my head, and then you stole my book!"

"You mean *my* book!" Clyde laughed. "I told Bridgewater you stole it, and she's promised to get it back for me. So the minute she takes it from you, it's going directly into my hands, and then…" Clyde made a series of ripping motions with his hands, accompanied by disgusting noises that made his two friends laugh.

He was clearly enjoying watching Sandy squirm when something caught his eye. "Wait a second! What's this?" he said lunging at her, but before she could respond, he wrenched her arm from behind her and yanked the book out of her hand. "Why do you still have this?" "Give it back to me, Clyde!" Sandy screamed.

"Give it back to me, Clyde!" Clyde mimicked as he walked away, flanked by his buddies. "No! Fair's fair, Sock-Stinks. This book is *mine*."

Sandy lost control, and rushed toward Clyde with all of her strength. Before she got to him, though, he threw the book to Bud. Sandy followed the path of the book in the air, and rushed for it, but it sailed through the air again into Bret's hands, while Sandy flailed uselessly for it, stuck in an evil game of keep-away.

"What do you *want*?" Sandy finally gasped. "We're past negotiations," Clyde said authoritatively. "Right now, I'm going to teach you a little lesson. You don't seem to get it, that you're stupid. And no one likes you, Spotty. Me most of all," he added, as he took the book from Bud and ripped out the first page.

Sandy screamed and rushed at him again. Clyde had anticipated this and simply tossed the book back to Bud, calling "Rip it!" The game of keep-away began again, with each boy tearing out a page before throwing it on to the next. When they didn't have the book, they busied himself with tearing the ripped out pages into little bits.

Sandy was helpless. The torn pages on the floor were

crumpled and scattered more by her frantic efforts to salvage the remains of the book. At last, she gave up and bent over double, crying as she tried to pick up the battered pieces on the ground.

"And they lived happily ever after, the end!" Clyde called out, laughing as he tore a big chunk from the back of the book. "Like my dad says, 'If you want something done right, you have to do it yourself.' I should've known Bridgewater would go soft on you, the old bat! Maybe you and *her* can be friends, Ugly." Clyde howled as he threw the leather binding at Sandy's bowed head.

He looked over to where Bret and Bud had been, wondering why they weren't yucking it up with him, and realized they were no longer by his side but were instead running spastically down the hall. He was about to yell after them when he heard a noise that made his blood freeze.

"Huh-hem!"

Though Clyde was a big guy for his age, Ms. Bridgewater still towered over him. She fixed on him a powerful, nasty glare.

"Well, Mr. Debrah!" she said without adding the accent to his name. "Was it not just two hours ago that you came to me on the verge of tears about your missing book? And now I find you ripping it to pieces!"

"I… er, what I mean to say is… this is all Sandy's fault!" Clyde's head swiveled comically from side to side as he looked around for help from someone, anyone.

"Really…" Ms. Bridgewater said slowly, looking down at Sandy sobbing on the floor.

Chapter Five

"Well… I mean, yeah, she stole it, remember?" Clyde asked nervously.

"Let me see if I have this correct…Ms. Stockings stole your book…"

"Yeah!" Clyde said helpfully, trying desperately to regain his confidence.

"I see, and now you've caught her here with it, is that right, Mr. Debrah?"

"Yes! Yes, that's exactly right!" Clyde said, nodding furiously.

"And upon retrieving the book from her, you decided the best punishment for her stealing it was to rip it up over her head? Is that so, Mr. Debrah?" she spat out.

"Well, er…ya know, um…I dunno…Yeah…I guess…sort of…" Clyde mumbled.

"I see. Well, good for you!" Ms. Bridgewater exclaimed with a smile and a pat on his shoulder. Sandy looked up for the first time, tears still streaming down her face, horrified to think Clyde was going to get away with yet another thing.

"Really?" asked Clyde, who was at least as shocked as Sandy was.

"Truly! In fact, because you have been such a valuable assistant in keeping the peace, I have decided to do you a very big favor!" Ms. Bridgewater replied, still beaming. Sandy noticed that her eyes looked weird, though, somehow fiery and rather cold at the same time. Clyde was oblivious, and began to sneer victoriously at Sandy when he wasn't batting his lashes innocently at Ms. Bridgewater.

"I was going to wait to tell you," Ms. Bridgewater began in

a confidential tone, "but in honor of this great service you've done for the school, I think I can let the cat out of the bag a day early..." She paused to allow Clyde's excitement to fully build before continuing. "I have taken the liberty of talking with the high school football coach and have informed him of your heartfelt desire to serve the drama department, as you've confided in me so many times. It was difficult at first – he thinks an awful lot of you – but I finally managed to convince him to let you go."

Clyde's sneer fled, and he visibly paled, but Ms. Bridgewater went on. "He was very sorry to lose you, of course, and to make sure he wouldn't change his mind and be tempted to try and guilt you into playing again...I went ahead and used some of my connections with the school board in order to pass a new rule that makes *all* eighth graders ineligible to participate in high school athletics this year. You're going to be seen as *quite* the trendsetter among your peers in the sports world here at our school, Clyde. Isn't that great? Congratulations! Now you are freed from your obligations to the football team, and are, from this day on, a very special member of the Drama Club!"

When Ms. Bridgewater finished, she looked down at Sandy and smiled sadly. Clyde stood open-mouthed, looking even dumber than usual, Sandy thought.

"But...this is my eighth grade year, Ms. Bridgewater, and they were going to let me play varsity football in the *high* school! I've been waiting my whole life to be on the varsity team, and it's actually come a year early!" Clyde whined, tears welling up in his eyes. "You can't do this to me! It's not fair! I'd be the first in my family to be on a varsity team a year early. I've never been the first of my family to do *anything*! I've got seven older brothers, and this was my chance—you can't *do* this to me!"

Ms. Bridgewater looked back at him kindly, and chuckled lightly. "Why, none of your brothers were in the Drama Club, Clyde, were they? So *that* will be your 'first,' hmm? And hold on to your hat, mister, because on top of that, I've created a special position for you. Because of your oft-stated devotion to the performing arts, which until now you have never been able to fulfill, you'll be the first person in the history of this whole school to be the Drama Club Assistant! Isn't that *exciting*?"

Clyde's eyes grew huge. "Good enough to get me laughed right out of town!" said he said, raising his voice.

"Well, Mr. Debrah! You have a funny way of showing your gratitude. Maybe you're just a little overwhelmed by the honor. I'm sure that everything will work out for the best. In the meantime, please report to my office tomorrow for a list of your new duties as the club's assistant."

"Duties! But..." Clyde started.

"That will be *all*, Mr. Debrah!" Ms. Bridgewater stated with a sudden glare that sent a shiver down Sandy's spine. Clyde shuffled away, muttering to himself.

The teacher watched him go, and when he was out of sight, she sat on the ground beside Sandy to help her pick up the torn pages. Neither of them said anything until every piece had been gathered.

"Can you really make it so Clyde can't play on that team?" Sandy finally asked softly.

Ms. Bridgewater laughed, shaking her head. "No, that's not really within my jurisdiction," she said, and then in a clever whisper she added, "But *he* doesn't know that."

Sandy smiled, but looking down at the torn pages in her hands, she felt herself starting to cry again.

"It's okay, Sandy. I'll tell your mother what happened," Ms. Bridgewater offered, rubbing her shoulders.

"It's not that," Sandy sobbed. "I didn't even get to find out what happened. I don't even know what this book is about!"

"I see," nodded Ms. Bridgewater. "Well, perhaps I could offer a solution. I've read this book before, Sandy. In fact, at one point in my life it was my favorite story. I had it memorized."

"Really?" Sandy shouted, as hope sprang back to life.

"Really," Ms. Bridgewater repeated. "But, I had forgotten all about it until you pulled it out of your bag." She looked down to the floor and picked up the leather cover, rubbing it lightly with her hands. "I haven't seen my copy of it in a long time, and it's been even longer since I've read it, but I can look for it, and even if I don't find it, I might be able to give you some idea of how it went. I actually remember quite a bit, I believe."

"When can we start?" asked Sandy, her hope growing.

"Well, I figure I will have the services of Mr. Debrah for at least the rest of the week before I have to turn him back over to the athletic department, so I won't require your assistance in cleaning my office," Ms. Bridgewater answered, picking herself off the floor.

"There still remains the matter of your detention, however, so I want you to report to me tomorrow afternoon at three o'clock. Then, I will tell you all I know about Asher and the Three B's." Ms. Bridgewater offered her hand to help Sandy up and then waved goodbye. "Try to come with an open mind. I'll see you tomorrow."

Sandy watched her go, and walked slowly down the empty hall, thinking about all the different things that had happened to her in the last 24 hours. She felt a strange but not unpleasant feeling in her stomach and somehow knew what it was. "This is what change feels like," she thought. "I've been flying solo long enough, and now things are about to change." She allowed herself a small, shy smile. For the first time in her life, Sandy was glad she hadn't found a hole to crawl inside.

Chapter Six

At two minutes past three o'clock, students were rushing through the hallways. On her way to Ms. Bridgewater's classroom, Sandy passed Clyde heading for the drama office with a bucket of cleaning supplies and a mop. He looked frazzled and was breathing very heavily out of his mouth like a wild horse. When he saw Sandy, he started to come over, but a small seventh grade boy, hoping to score some points with a "cool" upper classman, stopped him to ask when the varsity season started. Sandy watched the naïve boy receive the blows intended for her and couldn't help feeling slightly grateful.

"How is your mother, Sandy?" asked Ms. Bridgewater with concern when Sandy entered the classroom.

"She's all right, I guess," Sandy answered slowly. She trusted Ms. Bridgewater more now, but was still very sensitive, even protective, when she talked about her mom. "She sleeps a lot during the day, and then sometimes has trouble sleeping at night. Her doctor's given her some pills to take, but I don't think they work like they're supposed to. She's...not like she used to be, just sad all the time, and it's kind of like she doesn't know I'm around a lot of times."

"That's a pity."

"But lately things have been a little better, I think," Sandy added quickly. "I hope so, anyway. Were you friends with her, Ms. Bridgewater?"

"I'm not sure your mother would call me a friend—not now, anyway. At one point in time we pretended, though," Ms. Bridgewater said. "We met in a theatre workshop when we were very young, and it wasn't that we didn't like each other, but being close would have been impossible in that setting. She and I competed with each other for every role there was. I *despised* her when she beat me out for a part, and she despised *me* when I beat *her*...we fought a lot, and tried to sabotage each other whenever we got the chance.

"In hindsight, if I had spent as much time practicing as I did thinking of ways to ruin your mother's auditions, I might have gotten a few more roles." Ms. Bridgewater looked off into the corner of the room and smiled before continuing, "In truth, I was jealous of your mother. She was pretty, smart, and talented, and I hated her for it. But things didn't get really ugly until we both met John."

Sandy's eyes bulged, and her heart began beating out of her chest. She took a deep breath and swallowed before asking, "My *father*, John? What happened?"

Ms. Bridgewater smiled in an attempt to relieve some of the tension she knew Sandy felt, but thought it best to continue. "He was a charmer, and we both fell in love with him. The three of us did everything together. Your father seemed oblivious to the fact that two women were fighting for his affection, but then he was one of the best actors in our workshop, so it is difficult for me to say what he was really thinking.

"At any rate, in the end he chose your mother, as I'm sure you've deduced. But before that happened, he gave us both copies of that book, *Three B's for a Wannabe*. Your mother loved it, but I was a little bit insulted. I didn't want some silly book—I was *an actress*. Your mother understood, though, and I think her understanding, more than anything, is why she achieved so much."

"What happened to you?" Sandy asked suddenly.

"Me?" Ms. Bridgewater laughed. "Oh, I actually read the book many years after your father and mother were married. I remember sitting in my tiny, dark basement apartment in Chicago, getting ready to go to a rehearsal, when, out of nowhere, the book fell off of a crowded shelf. I gobbled up the entire book in no time."

"What about the rehearsal?" Sandy asked, horrified to think that Ms. Bridgewater would mess up such a glorious opportunity.

"I didn't go. In fact, I packed up all my stuff, and I took the first bus home," she said proudly.

"You just quit wanting to be an actress? Why?" Sandy squealed.

"Because as I read that book, I realized I didn't want to act anymore. When I really looked inside, I realized I hadn't wanted to act for a long time, but I felt like people would think I was crazy or a loser if I stopped after putting so much work into it. Then, I thought about what I had always really wanted to do, which was teach. I realized I was a teacher in my heart, so I had to start *being* one. I still love the theatre of course, but I wouldn't trade the rewards of teaching for all the roles on Broadway," said Ms. Bridgewater.

"That must have been some book," Sandy said with a sigh.

"It is. You should be very proud of your father."

"What do ya mean?" asked Sandy. She thought for a second then exclaimed, "Wait! You mean my father *wrote* that book?"

"That's right."

"Oh, wow! That's why…oh! My mother is going to absolutely flip when she finds out about all of this! Maybe she won't even be so mad about the fact that the book's destroyed now, do you think?"

Sandy grew quiet, lost in thought for a moment as she considered the man she remembered and what she'd gotten out of the book so far. She felt as if she'd solved one mystery, only to discover another, much bigger, waiting behind it.

Ms. Bridgewater stood up, reaching into her lower desk drawer to produce the book, identical to the one Clyde and his friends had destroyed. She held the book in her left hand and picked up a piece of chalk with her right.

"Telling your mother what you've learned from this mess is important," she said. "With that in mind, I am going to explain the book's lesson, what I know your father would have wanted you to know." She paused. "Can I trust you with my copy of the book? I'll give it to you to follow along."

"All right," Sandy said, her heart pounding with excitement.

"Do you think you're up for it?" asked Ms. Bridgewater.

"Yes, ma'am. But I have to warn you—Asher might have been the worst bee in his hive, but I'm the worst student in my grade."

Chapter Seven

"You're father's Three B's," Ms. Bridgewater said, clearing her throat. "You want to be an actress, is that correct, Sandy?"

"Yes, ma'am! More than anything!"

"Well, congratulations! You're already a success!" Ms. Bridgewater exclaimed, applauding.

"What do ya mean?" asked Sandy, feeling mocked by the gesture.

"I mean that you have achieved the goal you set for yourself—you're a wannabe actress. You've accomplished step one!" Ms. Bridgewater exclaimed, smiling broadly. She concentrated her gaze on Sandy, saying slowly, "Here's the trick: if you really want to succeed, you have to know what you are. You are an actress, Sandy, so you need to start thinking like one."

"But I've never acted in anything," Sandy replied, frowning.

"That doesn't matter right now. In fact, it doesn't matter if anybody else knows it—ever! You don't have to have proof to understand what kind of person you are." She paused, then said firmly, "Sandy Stockings, what are you?"

"I... I guess... I mean... I dunno," Sandy said looking down to the desk in front of her.

"Oh, Sandy, c'mon. What *are* you?

"Ms. Bridgewater..."

"Don't think, just say it!"

"I... I, guess I'm a..."

"With feeling!" Ms. Bridgewater laughed

"I'm an actress!" Sandy yelled, blushing.

"Very good!" cried Ms. Bridgewater. "That's the first B: BECOME. This is the step that takes place completely inside of you. While *imagining* yourself as an actress is very easy, actually *believing* you are can be very difficult, as you've just discovered. But having faith in yourself is incredibly important. 'Know yourself,' as the Greeks say. Remember when Asher woke up after discovering himself?"

"Yeah. He didn't know what to do," Sandy said.

"That's right. What to do next is the great dilemma of mankind. What did Asher do?" Ms. Bridgewater asked.

"He followed Felix around," Sandy responded.

"But why?"

"I guess because Felix knew more than he did."

"Yes, but why?" Ms. Bridgewater probed.

"Why did Felix know more?" Sandy said, starting to feel a bit confused.

"No. Why did he follow anybody? Why couldn't he just *ask* Felix? Or read a book about it?" Ms. Bridgewater asked.

Chapter Seven

"Because he was trying to get better. He couldn't have learned as much from an explanation, and it didn't sound like the hive had a library," Sandy said with a smile.

"I don't know about that. It was a pretty great hive, from what I recall," Ms. Bridgewater laughed. "But otherwise you're exactly right. You can only learn so much secondhand. You wouldn't trust a doctor to perform surgery after he had only had the procedure explained to him in a classroom, right? Firsthand experience is an important part of learning, and in our case, achieving our goals.

"That is why the second step is BE NEAR. This is the *active* step, one that requires an actual change in the way you do something. It could be as small as changing your routine, the every day way you live your life, or as big as moving to a different city, like I did when I decided to leave acting and come back to teach. But the bigger the goal, the bigger the step.

"Step two is probably the *scariest* step because, more often than not, the change requires something unfamiliar. And it can be hard to trust yourself with something you've never tried before. Working next to Felix was the hardest day of Asher's life, but that experience was necessary for his success. You'll never achieve anything if you don't start *doing* something," Ms. Bridgewater said.

"That makes sense," Sandy thought. "But how do you know if you're near the right things?"

"These steps are very simple, but they aren't an exact formula. It may take more than one try. That's where persistence comes in. But if you are going after a goal, the desire shouldn't be a problem.

"Look at Asher. He didn't stop after Felix; he kept going around to all the bees in his hive to learn. The purpose of the second step is to surround yourself with what you already know, and that is what you *are*," Ms. Bridgewater said. "My older brother played football for years. Have you ever been to a football game?" Ms. Bridgewater asked.

"No, ma'am," Sandy said.

"If you ever get the chance, I suggest it—even if you only go once. I used to love to go to my brother's games, but not to watch him play. I wish I had known about the Three B's back then to share them with him. He would have loved them. Though, to tell you the truth, part of me thinks he already knew them. You see, he was a fairly good player, but he wasn't the best. All his life he wanted to be quarterback, and he practiced all the time. But another boy in his class was an incredible athlete, just *gifted*. He didn't have to work as hard, and had twice the talent."

"Like the high-ranking bees in the book!" Sandy piped up.

"Exactly. Most people would have gotten the hint and tried working on another position, but my brother worked twice as hard. I enjoyed going to the games because I saw my brother on the sidelines during every play, utterly and completely focused on what was happening on the field. Most people thought he was crazy. He would literally go through the motions of every play with his hands. As far as he was concerned, he was on the field, and *he* was making every play.

"The third step is BE READY. It really combines the first two steps of thought and action. Asher was ready to take his place as the highest-ranking bee long before the meeting of the colony. He had been preparing himself the whole time he was learning from the other bees. Being ready helps to motivate your actions. It keeps your goal in focus so that you know how to BE NEAR.

"My brother got his chance on the field one rainy Saturday. The main quarterback was hit pretty hard, and was out of the game. The coach didn't even need to call my brother's name. He knew exactly what to do, and trotted to the field with his helmet on. The game wasn't the championship or anything, but he completed every play with so much intensity, you would have thought it was the Super Bowl. I don't remember if they won or lost, but that wasn't important. He was ready when his number was called.

"It occurs to me, that on *your* wannabe journey, the Drama Club would be a good start," Ms. Bridgewater said with a kind smile.

"I've wanted to be in the Drama Club since the first grade!" Sandy said bursting with joy.

Ms Bridgewater nodded and said, "Well, I think that will be a good goal to set for yourself, but remember extracurricular activities require certain grades for eligibility. I'd hate to lose a great actress due to a poor academic record."

"I'm no good at school, though, Ms. Bridgewater," Sandy said miserably. "I haven't done well for… a long time."

"I was an actress for fifteen years, only to start over in a completely different profession. I know you're a lot smarter than anybody has given you credit for, myself included. So I'm sure you're more than capable of making adequate grades. We improve when we apply ourselves. Your father wrote the story about Asher going from worst bee to the highest rank for a reason. He believed in his principles, and he knew they would work in any situation. Try using the Three B's."

Sandy couldn't remember the last time someone had complimented her intelligence. Somewhere along the line she had started listening to people when they called her "dumb." She saw herself in Asher and, bit by bit, excitement grew inside of her.

Ms. Bridgewater continued, "If you're an actress, you need to be near things that will help you. Step two, BE NEAR, requires a change in scenery and TAKING ACTION to achieve your goals."

Ms. Bridgewater took the chalk in her hand and started printing on the board. "Let's review. The Three B's for a Wannabe are:

BECOME
BE NEAR
BE READY

"Sandy, I need to leave for a few minutes, "Mrs. Bridgewater said. "Why not find the page in your book where you ended, and read what your dad had to say about The 3 B's. Or, rather, what Asher has to say!" she smiled. "The more ways you can hear this message, the better. One of the best tools in the learning process is repetition."

Sandy had been dying to open the book and didn't look up from it as Mrs. Bridgewater left the room and quietly closed the door.

BARRY LOWERED THE LIGHTS IN THE HIVE'S ASSEMBLY HALL AND ASHER USED A POINTER TO INDICATE EACH POINT ON THE SLIDE HE HAD HASTILY MADE FOR HIS PRESENTATION.

ASHER CLEARED HIS THROAT, CONFIDENT, BUT STILL A LITTLE NERVOUS FROM THE BIG BUZZ EARLIER. "THESE ARE THE 'THREE B'S FOR A WANNABE.' THEY'RE ALL ABOUT BECOMING WHO YOU REALLY ARE, WHO YOU <u>WANNABE</u>. GET IT?" HE

CHUCKLED NERVOUSLY, FEELING SOME RESISTANCE FROM THE CROWD, THOUGH HE COULD TELL THEY WERE PAYING ATTENTION, GIVING HIM A CHANCE.

"MENTALLY, YOU MUST BECOME THAT WHICH YOU ALREADY ARE," HE BEGAN AGAIN, AND INSTANTLY FELT MORE ASSURED, SO CERTAIN WAS HE OF THE PRINCIPLES THAT HAD CHANGED HIS LIFE. "THE GREAT THING ABOUT THIS FIRST STEP," HE CONTINUED, "IS THAT IT DOESN'T HAVE ANYTHING TO DO WITH ANYONE ELSE. IT DOESN'T MATTER IF ANYONE ELSE KNOWS WHO YOU WANNABE, AS LONG AS YOU KNOW IT. NO MATTER WHAT HAPPENS, THAT IS WHAT YOU ARE, AND NO SOUL ON EARTH CAN TAKE THAT AWAY FROM YOU. THIS MINDSET IS EASY TO ACCEPT AT FIRST, BUT IT WILL TAKE CONSTANT REPETITION TO KEEP IT UP WITH YOUR EVERYDAY LIFESTYLE."

"NEXT, TO BE NEAR IS TO SURROUND YOURSELF WITH THAT WHICH YOU ARE. IF YOU'RE A WANNABE ACCOUNTANT, YOU GOTTA FIND YOURSELF A GREAT ACCOUNTANT TO SHADOW AND SNEAK A FEW MINUTES ON THE CALCULATOR NOW AND THEN. IF YOU'RE A WANNABE OPERA SINGER, YOU NEED TO LISTEN TO OPERA, AND EVEN HANG OUT WITH A GREAT OPERA SINGER. IT'S HARD SOMETIMES TO ADMIT IT, BUT EVERYBODY NEEDS HELP SOMETIMES. I SURE DID, AS ALL OF YOU

KNOW," HE CHUCKLED SOFTLY. "SURROUNDING YOURSELF WITH THINGS TO ENCOURAGE YOU IS BETTER THAN TRYING TO DO EVERYTHING BY YOURSELF. YOU HAVE TO BE NEAR THOSE THINGS THAT ENCOURAGE YOUR EFFORTS. THEY ONLY NEED TO BE SMALL CHANGES AT FIRST, BUT THEY NEED TO REQUIRE YOUR ACTION. YOU CAN'T JUST THINK YOUR WAY INTO BEING WHAT YOU WANNABE.

"EVEN IF YOUR GOAL IS GIGANTIC, YOU HAVE TO START SOMEWHERE. BIG GOALS HAVE NATURAL OBSTACLES THAT ARISE ON YOUR WAY TO THEM. YOU CAN'T JUST WAKE UP ONE MORNING AND BE WHATEVER YOU WANNABE, OR AT LEAST YOU CAN'T BE THE BEST AT WHAT YOU WANNABE. YOU CAN'T EXPECT TO TACKLE THE BIGGEST OBSTACLE IMMEDIATELY AND BE SUCCESSFUL AT IT. YOU MUST ALLOW YOURSELF TO FLY A LITTLE FURTHER

EACH DAY, OR A LITTLE HIGHER EACH DAY, TACKLING THOSE OBSTACLES ONE BY ONE UNTIL YOUR ORIGINAL GOAL IS JUST THERE, READY FOR YOU, RATHER THAN BEING A HUGE, INTIMIDATING CHALLENGE."

ASHER LOOKED OUT INTO HIS AUDIENCE, WHO SAT AT RAPT ATTENTION. HE SMILED A LITTLE TO HIMSELF AND TURNED BACK WITH HIS POINTER TO THE SCREEN, POINTING TO BE READY. "THIS IS THE RISKY PART. YOU NEED TO KEEP YOUR MIND AND HEART IN A STATE OF "READINESS" SO THAT YOU CAN BE RIGHT THERE, STANDING WITH YOUR HAND ON THE DOORKNOB WHEN OPPORTUNITY KNOCKS. WHEN THE WORLD'S MOST BEAUTIFUL FLOWER PRESENTS ITSELF TO YOU, WITH ENOUGH POLLEN FOR A WEEK - OR WHAT THE HECK? FOR A MONTH! - YOU MUST BE ABLE TO SEE IT FOR WHAT IT IS, AND BE READY TO TAKE A CHANCE

ON AN OPPORTUNITY WHEN IT POKES ITS HEAD UP AND SMILES AT YOU. IF, INDEED, YOU HAVE BECOME WHO AND WHAT YOU TRULY ARE, AND HAVE SURROUNDED YOURSELF WITH THINGS THAT ENCOURAGE YOU TO REACH YOUR GOAL, THEN IT WILL ONLY BE A MATTER OF TIME UNTIL THE ANSWERS TO YOUR DREAMS ARE RIGHT THERE, STARING YOU IN THE FACE. SO YOU NEED TO BE READY TO STARE RIGHT BACK, COMPLETELY UNAFRAID."

A LOW BUZZ STARTED IN THE AUDIENCE. BEES ARE WIDELY KNOWN FOR A DISTINCT LACK OF REALLY COURAGE, ONLY PRETENDING TO BE FEARLESS - THEY'RE GENERALLY CONSIDERED ONE OF THE BULLIES OF THE INSECT WORLD - AND ASHER HAD WONDERED IF THIS STEP MIGHT NOT THROW THEM FOR A LOOP. "MAYBE YOU'RE WONDERING WHAT HAPPENS IF YOU LOSE COURAGE, JUST FOR A LITTLE WHILE, AND YOU

BLOW A CHANCE? OR IF YOU'RE NOT IN THE HIVE WHEN OPPORTUNITY COMES KNOCKING ON THE HIVE DOOR?"

"YES! YES, ASHER! WHAT HAPPENS THEN?" THE BEES BUZZED ANXIOUSLY, PREPARED FOR DISAPPOINTMENT.

ASHER SMILED KINDLY. "YOU NEED NOT FEAR, EVERYONE. YOU'LL SEE: CHANCES WILL KEEP COMING BY, BUT YOU SHOULD SNAP THEM UP WHENEVER YOU CAN. NO ONE WILL EVER BE FULLY PREPARED, BUT WHEN OPPORTUNITY COMES YOUR WAY, YOU'RE JUST GOING TO HAVE TO TAKE IT!"

SUDDENLY THE BEES' FRIGHT TURNED TO EXHILARATION, AND THEY ALL SALUTED ASHER WITH FLOWERS.

Chapter Seven

Ms. Bridgewater had quietly entered the room; Sandy had been too engrossed to even hear her. Suddenly she looked up and saw that the clock read six minutes to five o'clock. Her detention was over, and she knew she needed to hurry home.

"We still have that quiz tomorrow?" Sandy asked, carefully placing the book on Ms. Bridgewater's desk.

"Oh, yes," Mrs. Bridgewater replied, not hiding her surprise that Sandy remembered or had even noticed when she'd made the announcement in class.

"Well, then I'd better get home and get to work, huh?" Sandy said, hurrying out the door.

Chapter Eight

The sun had set by the time Sandy returned home, and her mother was already asleep on the living room couch. Sandy ran up the stairs and bulldozed her way through the clutter on the floor of her bedroom. After pushing aside all the clothes, she turned on her desk lamp. She had a lot of work to do if she planned on making a good grade on the quiz.

She knew she was capable; she just had to surround herself with the environment that would help her to succeed. "Be Near," Sandy thought, staring at a wadded sock draped over the lamp shade.

"How could anyone ever expect to get work done in a pig sty like this?" Sandy said aloud, surveying her room with a shudder.

A pile of crusty dishes sat in front of the television where she liked to eat.

Raggedy clothes were strewn all about the floor.

I Wanna Be...

Toys and books, CDs and tapes, were scattered around the room, most of them covered in dust or grime.

"I wannabe cleaner than this..." Sandy started to say, but stopped. The realization swept over her, and she began to laugh. "Wait! I AM cleaner than this!" she said with an eager giggle.

She found a trash bag hidden behind a broom in the closet, and began running around her room. She struck with an almighty force to the left and to the right. She found things that she had thought she'd lost forever, and threw out all kinds of trash with a disgusted, "Gross!" like cups where the Kool-Aid had sat so long it had evaporated, leaving a bright ring. Chicken bones, practically fossilized. Half-eaten candy bars. She shelved books and music, made her bed, threw practically her whole wardrobe into a basket, and struggled to carry it to the laundry room.

After about an hour, the room had fully changed. But Sandy didn't want to stop. She moved on to the kitchen, pulling all the dusty cleaning supplies from under the sink. She washed the dishes, polished the countertops, scrubbed the windows, and mopped the floor, humming softly all the while and dancing a little bit with the mop. A happier Cinderella never existed.

She tip-toed into the living room, and picked up around the couch where her mother had crashed. Mrs. Stockings never moved a muscle, deeply asleep as Sandy dusted and stacked, bringing a new sense of life and order to the room. She stopped short of vacuuming, but moved on to the den and her mother's room. When she finally finished, she was exhausted but had never felt so proud. All around her, her labor of love glistened. She took one last look at the good job she had done, then returned to her fresh, gleaming desk to start studying.

The next morning, Sandy woke up at dawn. She made up

her bed again and walked to the store to buy groceries with money she had found lying in nooks and crannies around the house while she was cleaning. She returned to make her mother breakfast and a nice, fresh pot of coffee.

Sandy had never attempted to wake her mother up before. Mrs. Stockings hadn't moved from the night before. Sandy stepped lightly to the couch with the tray of food and hot coffee, extending a hand to rub her mother's shoulders gently.

Mrs. Stockings groaned and blinked several times. "What is it, Sandy, something wrong?" she asked in a thick, raspy voice.

"I made you some breakfast, Mama, and some coffee. I just wanted to wake you up to tell you goodbye," Sandy said softly.

"Goodbye? Where are you going?" questioned her mother. "What time is it?"

"Almost seven thirty," Sandy said, seeing that her mother was starting to fall back to sleep. She didn't want to be rude, but she wanted her mother to see what she had done. She lightly tapped her awake again. "Aren't you going to eat your breakfast, Mama?"

"No, sweetie, I'm not really very hungry. Have a good day at school," Mrs. Stockings said, dozing off again.

Sandy stood up and moved toward the door. She could see she wasn't going to get the response that she had hoped for, but she realized that it didn't really matter. Sandy knew she was a good girl and a good daughter. She ate her mother's breakfast while looking once more at her nice, clean house, then jogged to school, thinking happily about how she was using her father's Three B's.

Chapter Nine

The weeks passed by, and Sandy raced to catch up with them. Because she hadn't participated in any aspect of being a student for years, she found that keeping up with all of the reading, homework, and studying for tests was a full-time job. Her change didn't come as fast as Asher's had. If her father had still been with her, Sandy would probably have critiqued the story at this point. Instead she complained to her new friend, Ms. Bridgewater.

"What am I doing wrong?" she relentlessly asked.

"*Be* patient," Ms. Bridgewater always answered.

"Very funny," Sandy would mutter.

The most disappointing event, however, was the first math quiz she got back, which was a total failure. Even though she studied harder than she ever had, a night's work couldn't make up for her years of poor habits. She didn't get *any* answers right, but she had done some of the work properly, which gave her partial credit. Still, that didn't count, either, since she was pretty sure Ms. Bridgewater had taken it easy on her.

Sandy crumpled her test and sat in the back of the room pouting for the remainder of the class. As she slouched out, Ms. Bridgewater kindly reminded her of the grades she would need to have to get in to the Drama Club.

"How about moving up closer to the front of the classroom, Sandy? It might help you to focus." Sandy nodded, and took her advice the next day.

Slowly, Sandy's grades in all of her classes improved. She found that she loved reading, ravenously devouring novels and plays in English, the true stories of important men and women in history, experiments and case studies in her science textbook, and even the story problems in math. "An actress' job is to tell stories, to make them come alive," she'd think. "So the more stories I know, the better I can tell 'em!"

Sandy felt more confident every time she completed the work her teachers assigned, instead of nervously thinking of excuses before each class. Soon her teachers were treating her with more respect, and Rachel, a girl in her math class, actually asked Sandy for help one day. It felt like the first time that someone her own age had talked to her without saying anything mean.

Even Sandy's temper cooled. She didn't have Clyde to worry about anymore, at least. He seemed to have turned over a new leaf since he found out he was still on the varsity team. The idea of not playing had been such a torment to him that he went out of his way to avoid getting into trouble, at least with Sandy.

At home, Sandy started to notice that her mother didn't have as many remembering days. The boxes of memories had not been

Chapter Nine

back to the living room since Sandy discovered *Three B's for a Wannabe*. Mrs. Stockings kept the house clean, washed clothes, and even cooked dinner, most nights. Once in awhile, she'd order a pizza and eat a couple of slices with Sandy while they watched favorite old movies on TV. The fridge was filled with groceries, and the house was filled with music. Mrs. Stockings called the garbage company to put her back on their route, and paid to have them clear the trash out of the backyard; it took a small bulldozer to get everything cleared!

Mrs. Stockings started doing things that a normal mother would. She took Sandy shopping, buying her a whole new set of clothes—including a dress and some skirts! Everything was beginning to go well, and Sandy was shocked to find October fourteenth, tryout day, waiting for her as she rolled out of bed one morning.

Sandy ran down the stairs, eager to start the new day, but as she did, a pang of anxiety shot through her body. The light was on in the living room, and the boxes of memories were strewn across the floor. Her mother was tearing through the contents, throwing papers and pictures into the air.

Sandy's heart stopped when she realized the velvet bag was sitting out on the coffee table, its contents emptied in a pile. She finally saw all the pictures of her father that had been missing from the walls. Sandy stood on the last stair without moving, waiting for her mother to notice her. Mrs. Stockings didn't look up, though.

"Where is the *book*, Sandy?" Mrs. Stockings yelled.

"I can explain..." Sandy started to say, but it was too late. Her mother charged over to her with a wild glare.

I Wanna Be...

"I don't care why you took it, and I don't care what you did with it while you had it, I just want it back—NOW!" Mrs. Stockings stuck out her hand as if Sandy were carrying the book with her.

"I don't have it," she answered, tears welling up in her eyes.

"Get it!" Mrs. Stockings screamed.

"I can't! I can't! I'm sorry! I'm sorry. I took it to school, and this boy stole it, and then… and then… he ripped it up!" Sandy whispered through her sobs.

Mrs. Stockings shrunk back in horror. "What? He ripped it up?" She walked backwards a few feet before turning and collapsing on to the couch.

Sandy tried to speak, but no words came out. She walked slowly to the couch and wrapped her arms around her mother, crying, "I'm sorry, Mama. It was an accident! I know who wrote the book! I didn't mean to take it. If I had known, I would never have let it leave the house. It just seemed like such a good book, and I never got to really know who he was, so having him with me was nice, is all!" Sandy could see that her mother's eyes were shut tightly, "Don't go to sleep! Please! What can I do? I'll do anything! Please, please, I'm sorry! What can I do?"

"Go to your room and stay there," Mrs. Stockings said without opening her eyes.

"How long should I wait?" Sandy asked.

"Until I tell you," Mrs. Stockings said coldly.

"But tryouts for the play are today, remember? And I can't miss, or I won't be in the play," Sandy gasped.

"You should have thought about that before you stole my

book!" Mrs. Stockings yelled, her eyes flying open and full of fire.

"I'm sorry!" Sandy screamed.

"Please, just go to your room. I want to be alone," Mrs. Stockings sighed, closing her eyes again.

Sandy walked away, giant tears rolling down her cheeks. She climbed the steps into her room and slammed the door. Her morning had turned into a nightmare, plain and simple. She jumped back in bed and pinched herself in an effort to wake up from the horrible dream. She tossed and turned, listening for her mother's footsteps on the stairs, praying she'd relent and let her go to the tryouts.

Everything was silent. Sandy got up and walked to the door to listen, but could only hear a faint weeping sound. She turned around and started to walk back to her bed to make it up, but stopped. A rush of anger filled her, and her heart sank down into her stomach. She wasn't going to get to try out! All the work, all the studying, cleaning, and acting polite for nothing!

Sandy kicked the bedpost hard. She walked over to her closet; everything was in perfect order—the dresses were to the left, then the skirts, pants, blouses, t-shirts, sweaters, and jackets all the way to the right. She thought about the time it took to organize everything, and the effort it took to keep it that way.

She felt sick. In one quick dart, she started grabbing clothes and throwing them all over her vacuumed floor. She kicked her shoes out of order, and flew by her desk, knocking everything over with a sweep of her arm. She ripped all the books from the shelves, and flung her sheets off her bed. She picked up stuffed animals, and hurled them against the walls of her room.

I Wanna Be...

Sandy blew through the space like a tornado, and did her best to destroy everything as she went. She couldn't hear anything except her own powerful rage. She screamed, shouted, cried, and moaned until she had nothing left to knock over. Her room was in shambles, just as it had been for years. But instead of feeling good about getting her old life back, Sandy still felt sick to her stomach.

She sat down on her now bare mattress she'd pulled halfway off the bed and waited for something to happen. She had worked so hard, and for what? Sandy felt empty. She didn't want to give up or to go back to the way things were before, but what was the point? Why couldn't she have what she wanted?

Breathing hard at first, but then slowly calming down, Sandy sat on the edge of her bed for hours, thinking about her life. After awhile, it started to seem a little less hopeless. Her dream of being an actress was still there, even if she would have to wait to make it come true.

Sandy thought hard, trying to imagine what her next obstacle would be. If opportunities really were like Ms. Bridgewater said, then she would have another one in the future. She lay back on a corner of the mattress and closed her eyes for a minute, but then opened them quickly when she heard a noise downstairs.

It was knock on the front door, something she realized she hadn't heard for years. She waited, but couldn't hear anything until the knock sounded again. Silence returned, then the knock. Whoever was at the door wasn't going away, so Sandy opened the door to her room and slowly crept down the steps. Near the bottom, she was shocked to see Ms. Bridgewater standing in the doorway, Sandy's mother blocking her path into the living room.

Chapter Nine

"Estelle. It's been a long time," Ms. Bridgewater said slowly.

"Carla..." Mrs. Stockings responded coldly. Both women stood in silence, and Sandy crept an inch closer. "Go back to your room," Mrs. Stockings said without turning around. "This will be a private discussion."

Sandy could see that her mother was in no mood for a response, so she skipped up the stairs as quietly as she had come down them and hid out of sight on the landing. When the door clicked shut, Mrs. Stockings turned her back and walked back into the living room. "I don't know what has happened, Carla, and I don't really care. I just know I don't want you filling my daughter's head with that 'Three B' nonsense," she sneered.

Ms. Bridgewater remained firm, "You know, Estelle, this reminds me of a story of a little girl who wanted to act so desperately..."

"Oh, please, Carla! You never could leave well enough alone!" Mrs. Stockings snapped. She turned around to face Ms. Bridgewater, her chestnut hair shaking in every direction. "You're as bad as John was, do you know that? Telling stories and filling young people with crazy ideas about following stupid dreams. Where did it get him? Do you see him here with his family?"

Ms. Bridgewater took a step closer, "He didn't die because he didn't love you, Estelle."

"What would you know about it? Were you there?" Mrs. Stockings cried. And then in a strange smile she continued, "I know what you think—because I think it, too! If only he had chosen *you*, he'd still be alive."

"Estelle!"

"But that's just it! He *did* choose you, Carla," Mrs. Stockings laughed.

Ms. Bridgewater looked horrified, "What are you talking about?"

"Do you think I wanted to come back here? I was on my way to a great career, Carla. But John wanted to raise a family, or so he said, and he thought this was a better place for that than New York. And then, suddenly, here we were: John working construction, me at home with Sandy, wondering where the last seven years had gone, scheming all the time about how I could get us all out of here and back to the city. Then one day he comes home, all excited to tell me he's gotten a "real" job. Here I was trying every way I could think of to get us *out* of this town, and he's setting up his retirement—as a teacher… just like you," Mrs. Stockings scowled. "Oh, don't think we didn't hear about you—coming back, followin' your dream, and whatnot."

"Thanks to him, I was able to do that."

"And don't think he didn't know it," Mrs. Stockings said, crossing her arms and flopping down on the couch.

Ms. Bridgewater walked over and stood beside her. "I came over here to tell you a story, but if our visit is going to upset you, I'll go." Ms. Bridgewater started for the door.

Mrs. Stockings fell for the trap, and sighing heavily, she replied, "No, go ahead, Carla. Stay. Tell me your little story."

Ms. Bridgewater returned and took her seat with a smile. "I was saying how much Sandy's situation reminds me of a young actress I used to know. Now, this girl was not your average adolescent with a dream. She knew what she was and that she was destined for greatness. As soon as she graduated from high school, she was off to New York to try out for the first play she could find. She was not content with her hometown's little dinner theatres. No, she was determined to have her name glittering in lights, to be around the real talent—the big stars.

"She went to a theater off-off Broadway and sat next to a dozen trained actresses, all competing for the same part. No one knew her, but anonymous or not, she knew that she was an actress and wasn't going to let the others stand in her way. She held her head high."

Ms. Bridgewater stopped, sighing before she continued. "Unfortunately, without an agent or connections, and only limited experience, the girl not only didn't get the part, she wasn't even allowed to try out! She went to the parking lot and sat down on the curb, waiting until all the cars were gone—except one.

"It was getting dark, but eventually the tired, old director stepped out of the building. He hesitated when he saw the girl. He didn't even wait for her to introduce herself before he started explaining that the decision had not been up to him, and that if he had his way all the girls would have gotten a chance to try out.

"She knew he was lying to make her feel better. Despite her rejection, she still felt a need to spend all of her time learning around the great actors in the professional theatre. She asked for any job she could have to just be near the other actors. The director liked her enthusiasm and made her the curtain girl, in charge of, but not limited to, opening and closing the curtains at appropriate times."

Mrs. Stockings had finally regained some color in her face

and sat on the couch, trying hard not to look interested in what Ms. Bridgewater had to say.

"There she sat, night after night," Ms. Bridgewater's calm voice continued, "watching another girl practice the lead role in a play that was so obviously written for our curtain girl. But she wasn't content with just watching. She was determined to learn; she wanted to be ready. So that's exactly what he girl did. She learned the entire play. She learned the stage directions and all the lines. She'd sometimes get yelled at by the actors because in certain scenes she would forget that she was in the wings, not onstage, and the actors could hear her saying their lines from backstage. In her heart, she was the lead actress, whether anyone ever knew it or not.

"After a couple of months, the opening night came and went. But no one was ready for what was about to happen. The lead actress was a TV star who was making her first foray into acting in live theater. She had been okay in rehearsal, but in performance, she was so nervous that she forgot half her lines, missed cues, and stepped on other actors' lines. While everyone in the production had hoped that the opening night excitement might encourage the star to give her best performance, they were wrong. And the reviews of her performance were *brutal*, so much so that the lead actress' agent called the next day, telling the director she'd fallen deathly ill with a mysterious illness that no one had ever heard of and would have to quit the show.

"The understudy was suddenly deathly afraid to perform in the role after reading the reviews. She believed everyone would hate her if she couldn't carry the show, so she decided perhaps the theatre wasn't all it was cracked up to be and ran off with one of the stagehands."

Mrs. Stockings smiled and shook her head.

Ms. Bridgewater continued, "The very tired, very old, and now very stressed-out director was at his wits' end. No one could learn all of the lead actress' lines in a night. He couldn't just close the show, even temporarily, without lawsuits and who knows what-all. He had all but given up, when the curtain girl approached him.

"'I can do it, sir,' she said confidently. 'I'm ready.'

"'Surely not,' the director thought. He couldn't let a stagehand carry the play. But soon, after hearing her act out the whole first act of the play–not just the lead's lines, but every single character's–he decided she was the best of all his very limited options. He wisely selected her to take the lead in that night's performance, and he knew that she was, indeed, more than just a lowly curtain girl when the play got a standing ovation, and the audience screamed 'Bravo!' at the girl's curtain call. The talk in the lobby was all about a new star being born, destined for Broadway. 'You'd better hold on to her,' everyone told the director. 'She's going to be a huge star!'

"The curtain girl was an enormous success. She had become, been near, and been ready. I can even remember sitting in the audience with John. You made him very proud, Estelle Stockings. You really were magnificent."

Mrs. Stockings looked at Ms. Bridgewater with eyes glassy with tears but glowing with an inner light that had been lost for many years. "You always were a very wise woman. I should have known you were filling Sandy's head with John's words when she woke me up to eat breakfast." Her smile grew as she looked around the house. "Look at this place, Carla. It's spotless. That's her. It wasn't…like this…for a long time."

Ms. Bridgewater laughed. "Well, Estelle, if I didn't know you any better I'd think you were proud."

"I just don't want my girl getting hurt like I did, Carla. The world can be such an awful place for someone who's blindly following a dream. She doesn't deserve that pain."

They both grew quiet for a minute. Then Ms. Bridgewater broke the silence. "I understand the *home*, too, can be quite an awful place for someone following a dream—or just trying to grow up, in fact."

Mrs. Stockings whimpered. "Carla, you don't understand! I can't do it! I see his face every time I look at that girl."

Ms. Bridgewater answered loudly, "'That girl' is your daughter, and she is as special a person as you will hope to find, Estelle. John died four years ago. But if I remember, you had the pleasure of ten by his side. What would he think of you sleeping your life away while his daughter is trying to make something of herself? You need to start thinking about the people who are still around, Estelle."

Mrs. Stockings whimpered again, "But, Carla, John…"

"John is *dead*!" Ms. Bridgewater proclaimed loudly. And the sooner you realize that he doesn't need you anymore, the better. Sandy is *starving* for your attention. What's happened to you? That little girl loves you more than anything in this life, and you haven't stayed awake for the last four years long enough to notice."

"Do you know how he died?" Estelle asked suddenly.

"What?"

Chapter Nine

"Do you know how John died?"

"He was in a car accident."

"He was going to talk to you. We had a fight. I wasn't happy here. I wanted to go back to the city, back to the theatre. Sandy was young, just 6 years old. We started yelling...*I* started yelling. I told him I wanted to move, that I was sick of this town. I said I wanted to act again, and not in some dumb little dinner theater. He started coming down on me with those same Three B's. You never could say the word 'want' around John. I was raving! I told him that if he *wanted* a housewife so much, he should've married you!

"I think somehow he knew I was right. He sort of stormed out of here...He was gone for hours. When the police officer came to the door, I just knew immediately what had happened. But I wanted to know where. And he was less than a mile from your house, Carla. He was going to leave me."

"Is that what you think, Estelle?" Ms. Bridgewater gasped. "Is that what you've thought, all these years?"

"It's the truth. I know it." Mrs. Stockings said, looking away.

"John *did* come by my house that night," Ms. Bridgewater began, staring down to the floor and the boxes of her old rival's memories. "But it wasn't to tell me he loved me. He had gotten accepted to teach at the school; that's true. But what you don't know is that he had been talking to me about starting a theater company in town *for you and me*, where we could work together and do the kind of plays *you* wanted to do."

Ms. Stockings looked up. "What?"

"I didn't really like the idea at first. There was a lot between you and me that we would have had to get out of the way. But the more I talked to John, the more I realized it was a pretty great idea. And the more I realized how much he loved you."

"So what did he say to you?" Mrs. Stockings managed to ask.

"He told me about the fight, and asked if I could handle starting the company alone," Ms. Bridgewater said, looking deeply into Mrs. Stockings' eyes. "I was also supposed to inform the school board of his decision."

"His decision?" Mrs. Stockings said.

"John decided that it wasn't fair of him to clip your wings. He was coming home to take you and Sandy away, back to the city."

"What?"

"I knew he was right, but I didn't like it. I felt cheated somehow. I didn't want to hear about you succeeding again. I guess that jealous classmate still lived inside me, wanting to see you fail. The point is that John left my house excited to go home to see you and Sandy. When I heard what happened, I…I didn't know what to do," Ms. Bridgewater's eyes started to water. "So I never did anything. I never said anything. I'm so sorry for that, Estelle, especially since I know now how you felt."

Mrs. Stockings stared ahead at nothing, her face frozen in confusion. "He was coming home?" she finally said, choking back her tears.

"Yes," Ms. Bridgewater whispered.

"And… and he was happy?" Mrs. Stockings asked, biting her lower lip.

"Very," Ms. Bridgewater smiled.

Chapter Nine

"Oh, Carla, I can't believe it," Mrs. Stockings smiled, leaning in to hug Ms. Bridgewater. "I'm so glad to be wrong!" The two women sat there for awhile, rocking back and forth, hugging through their tears.

Finally, Ms. Bridgewater looked down to her purse and remembered the special delivery she had brought. "Here. I brought this for Sandy first, but I owe you the apology, so…here." Ms. Bridgewater handed Mrs. Stockings a finely worn leather bound copy of *Three B's for a Wannabe*.

"It's my fault that boy ripped up your book. I've been so angry with you for so long. I took it out on your daughter, and I would have continued to if it wasn't for this darn book. I'm so sorry, Estelle. I should've been there for you. I've been selfish, but I've changed. Please, let me prove…"

"Shhh. It's all right. You're here now, and that's what's important," Mrs. Stockings held the book close to her chest. And through tears of shame and love, she called to her daughter, "Sandy! Sandy come here!"

Sandy walked slowly down the stairs, as afraid of her mother's anger as she was of her tears; she was unprepared to react to the huge, warm hug from her mother.

"I'm so sorry," Mrs. Stockings said, holding Sandy's face in her hands. "Can you ever forgive me for the way I've treated you? I've been a terrible mother. Things are going to be different around here. No more sleeping our lives away, I promise. I'm so sorry."

Sandy nodded to acknowledge her mother's apology, then buried her face in her mother's neck again. She could feel the loving warmth she had once known in her mother slowly coming back and smiled, believing that her mother had truly changed.

After a thousand hugs and a few more tears, Sandy's mother turned to Ms. Bridgewater. "Can she still audition?"

"That's actually why I came. It's almost three o'clock. Sandy needs to be in the auditorium now!" Ms. Bridgewater said.

"Aren't you going to run the auditions?" Sandy asked.

"No, I am not. I've decided to take the rest of the afternoon off," Ms. Bridgewater said happily.

"But who is judging the try-outs?" Mrs. Stockings asked.

"My assistant in the high school has taken the job for the day. So Sandy will get a fair audition without any bias one way or the other," Ms. Bridgewater said with a wink.

"Assistant?" Mrs. Stockings asked.

"Only temporarily. I'm afraid she's leaving soon. I don't know what I'm going to do when she leaves—I have way too much work. If only I knew someone qualified, who actually knew the theatre..." Ms. Bridgewater said slyly, smiling at Mrs. Stockings.

"I imagine you can find someone who would love another chance to work near the stage again," Mrs. Stockings laughed.

Sandy looked at the two women , and could finally picture what she couldn't before: Her mother and Ms. Bridgewater hanging out as friends.

Sandy picked herself up, bowed to her teacher, and kissed her mother. Then she grabbed her book bag and walked quickly to the door.

"Break a leg!" both women called out to her.

Sandy was out the door when she turned back, poking her head in and smiling wider than anyone had ever seen her smile before. "If I don't get a part, I'll be proud to be the curtain girl, just like my Mama," she said.

Ms. Bridgewater and Mrs. Stockings were shocked. They had no idea she had been listening all along.

Sandy giggled with satisfaction. "And if I do get it, Mama, you can help me memorize my lines! This is going to be great either way! And don't worry Ms. Bridgewater, I'll 'be ready.' I mean, I AM ready!"

About the Authors

John Jacobs, born in Portsmouth, Ohio, was both the youngest and middle child in his family. For eight years, he was the youngest of three children, but then, within fourteen months, two other siblings arrived, making him the middle child. Three years after his father passed away, his mother remarried, and her new husband brought ten children to the family! Apart from losing his bedroom when the two clans joined, everyone in the family had a great life together.

John graduated from Ohio University in 1972 with a degree in education. He taught elementary school for five years while earning his Masters degree in reading and learning disability from Purdue University. In 1977, John took a leave of absence from teaching to pursue his administrator's license so he might fulfill another dream of becoming an elementary school principal. He never formally returned to the educational field.

John spent twenty-five years with a Fortune 500 company until, at the age of fifty, he decided to follow another dream, owning his own company. He started Sataria, a very successful warehouse and distribution company.

Today, while running Sataria with his wife Ramona and sister Helen, John is pursuing another dream: he is a passionate wannabe writer and motivational speaker who helps those who do not have confidence in themselves. John believes that everyone has what it takes to succeed when they have someone to mentor, motivate, and believe in them.

Daniel Jacobs was born on top of Lookout Mountain, Tennessee in 1983. He's the youngest of three boys, and we'll say the best looking. At 6'5" tall, he's a stalk among men. Daniel graduated from the University of Tennessee at Chattanooga where he earned a bachelors degree in English - Writing and a minor in Anthropology. He resides today in a small house with a leaky roof, spending much of his time reading and talking to himself. He's a nice guy deep down, and loves to hear a good story.